A MESSAGE FROM CHICKEN HOUSE

Horrid handkerchiefs were a big hazard in my childhood, along with sneezes, coughs and other nasty habits from all the kids in my class! But, of course, laughter is infectious too, and Alice's incredible germs are sure to cheer you up. You'll love this wonderful adventure from the irresistible new talent Gwen Lowe, who knows a thing or two about viruses in real life. Watch out: you may not be able to stop laughing out loud!

BARRY CUNNINGHAM
Publisher
Chicken House

ALICE DENT AND THE INCREDIBLE GERMS

GWEN LOWE

Chicken House

2 Palmer Street, Frome,
Somerset BA11 1DS

Text © Gwendolyn L. Lowe 2018
Illustrations © Sarah Horne 2018

First published in Great Britain in 2018
Chicken House
2 Palmer Street
Frome, Somerset BA11 1DS
United Kingdom
www.chickenhousebooks.com

Gwendolyn L. Lowe has asserted her right under the Copyright, Designs and
Patents Act 1988 to be identified as the author of this work.

British Library Cataloguing in Publication data available.

PB ISBN 978-1-910002-91-9
eISBN 978-1-911490-15-9

To my fantastic foursome:
for Cait, my favourite animal magnet,
for Phil, the perfect partner for all weathers,
for Ian, who knows the secret of happiness,
*and for Beatrix, who turned out **so much***
nicer than I expected when she grew up.

CHAPTER ONE
Number Nine Nettle Close

Mr and Mrs Dent were the sort of parents who didn't much like children.

'They're such grubby little creatures, always picking their crusty little noses and spreading germs and mess everywhere,' declared Mrs Dent that morning.

Dangling daringly out of the kitchen window, she extended her best long-handled grabber and expertly plucked their daily newspaper from the mailbox on the gate.

Mrs Dent never went outside; not if she could help it.

'It's a shame there aren't more fantastic parents like us, always on top of dirt and diseases,' she continued smugly, shaking a bottle of disinfectant into a foaming fizz. Soon the paper was drenched and Mrs Dent thrust it into the hot oven to toast.

Her words and the warm fumes nearly made Alice Dent choke.

Alice was sitting very quietly at the kitchen breakfast table in Number Nine Nettle Close, pretending that she was invisible. She was good at doing this; sometimes her parents forgot about her for hours at a time.

But that wasn't going to last, not today.

And very soon Alice knew she was going to be in the worst trouble on the planet.

All because she had a cold.

If I sneeze, I'm dead! she thought in panic, pinching her nose as she forced down her over-boiled egg. *Perhaps they won't notice*, she consoled herself. But this seemed unlikely, especially because she had to keep diving under the table to wipe her nose.

'Manners!' barked Mr Dent sharply, as Mrs Dent

took the sterilized paper out of the oven and handed it to her husband.

'Sorry,' muttered Alice, now stifling a cough. There was no way she could have guessed that these symptoms were the first sign of the strange and incredible world-changing events to come. And not knowing that was a great pity, because right now Alice could seriously do with being cheered up.

Meanwhile, Mrs Dent bustled around the kitchen, boiling shoelaces and polishing the soles of Mr Dent's work boots. She certainly didn't believe in changing the world. She thought that was a very dangerous idea.

'Those boots look just so, poppet,' said Mr Dent approvingly, lifting his head out of the smoking newspaper as Mrs Dent threaded the laces back in a perfect pattern. They smiled at each other fondly.

Alice hid her face and tried not to be sick. Her parents were perfectly matched. While Mrs Dent was ferret-like, sharp-nosed and keen on clean, Mr Dent was large and brawny and zealous about law and order. He liked things just so. 'Everything ship-shape and Bristol fashion,' he would say, sliding his strong arms into his protective suit for another day in pest control. Nothing made him happier than wiping out a big wasps' nest or exterminating a few cockroaches.

In truth, the worst thing that had ever happened to Mr and Mrs Dent was having a child. Alice wasn't best pleased about this either, although she tried not to mind too much.

Alice had interesting blue eyes with amber flecks and had to take five showers and soapy baths every day, more if Mrs Dent insisted. In fact, over her eleven years, Alice had been through so many showers and baths that she was surprised she hadn't shrunk to being smaller than average size. And she'd washed her long curly hair so much with strong soap that she was sure the colour was fading into streaks of blonde and ginger-brown.

She sighed. It wasn't fair that she had another cold. She really did try to stay neat and clean, even if she wasn't very good at it. And how could she have picked up any germs? She hadn't seen anyone. Her parents hadn't even let her go to school for a week because of the note sent home about pupils with stomach upsets.

'I say – that chap's certainly hit the ground running,' Mr Dent said suddenly. His voice was full of approval as he turned the slightly charred pages of the paper.

Oh no! Hastily, Alice squashed her nose to trap another sneeze. And, as if things weren't bad enough already, her parents were now going to go on about the new Best Minister for Everything Nicely Perfect again. They'd talked about nothing else all week.

'He's the best thing since sliced bread,' continued Mr Dent, as Mrs Dent lovingly buttered his toast. 'His ideas are marvellous, just what this country needs.'

'He's brilliant! And doesn't he look smart?' exclaimed Mrs Dent, stopping her spreading and peering over Mr Dent's shoulder. 'I wonder if I can get a signed photo of him?'

As Mrs Dent scooped the newspaper up to the light, Alice caught sight of the new Best Minister's face. She had glimpsed smaller news photos of him before, perfectly dressed in flawless suits. But this was the first time she had seen his features close-up, clear and sharp.

Alice studied the picture with growing unease. The Best Minister's eyes were like burning black pits dug into his pale skin, but it was his expression that made her feel like she'd swallowed an ice cube whole.

Something, some trick of the light perhaps, had turned it into a sinisterly perfect wax-like mask – and for some reason this made a chilly hand of dread squeeze her heart.

'They say that he's got big plans. He's going to cull cats, turn ice cream vans into mobile banks and outlaw orange clothes,' Mr Dent told them.

'Quite right too, orange is such a loud colour,' mused Mrs Dent. 'Myself, I prefer pink; you can't go wrong with a nice soft pink.'

'And apparently he's determined to stamp out children getting disgusting infections –so he's planning to ban lots of things like birthday parties.'

'An excellent idea!' approved Mrs Dent.

Alice wondered how stopping parties could stop germs. It sounded more like the new Best Minister was stamping out fun.

'He's forbidden all giggling in schools too. Any children who giggle will have to be reported at once to their headteacher for immediate punishment.'

'What a man!' swooned Mrs Dent, her eyes shining.

That proves it, thought Alice crossly. *He's definitely trying to make us miserable.*

'And he's getting the police to track down smelly

and dirty children. Those in charge are doing a fantastic job of taking them away from their hopeless parents and teaching them how to wash.'

'That's great news!' Mrs Dent nodded approvingly.

'Yes, that should sort out those niffy nippers. See how lucky you are to have such good parents, child?'

Alice boiled with rage. But she couldn't respond, her nose was dripping badly now and she was going to . . .

Oh no! Panicking, Alice dived hastily under the table again, stifling the sneeze just in time.

I can't bear much more of this, she muttered to herself. She was sick of trying to hide coughs and colds. She had thought things might get better when she got older but instead everything just seemed to be getting worse.

'It's about time something was done, the state of some of the little germ-spreaders you see nowadays!' Mrs Dent smugly adjusted the baby-pink headscarf that she always wore over her short brown hair. Then her expression changed. She leant towards Mr Dent.

'These rules . . . clamping down on germs and no giggling . . . especially no giggling . . . you don't think he's worried about the pie Russ coming back?' she whispered, so low that Alice could hardly hear her. She wasn't even sure Mrs Dent had actually said 'pie Russ', but that's what it sounded like.

Mr Dent went white.

'No, surely not . . .'

Mrs Dent gripped the table, her knuckles turning as pale as the snowy tablecloth.

'It would be the worst thing ever . . . can you imagine?' she whispered, her eyes wide and fearful.

'What's a pie Russ?' Alice spoke without thinking. She was breaking the house rule about children being seen and not heard, but she really wanted to know.

Her father threw Mrs Dent a warning look.

'We shouldn't talk about things like that in front of the child, poppet.'

He swivelled crossly to face Alice.

'And you should stop sticking your pesky little nose into things that don't concern you.'

Alice ground her teeth in frustration. This was a mistake – it made her cough.

Alarmed, Mr Dent peered at her more closely.

'Is your nose running? Have you . . . have you got a COLD?' he demanded fearfully.

Alice could have kicked herself. But it was too

late anyway; she couldn't hold it back any longer.

She was going to—

'AAAATISSSHOOOOO!'

'ARRRGH! GERMS!'

Mr Dent ran to the sink and stuck his head under the tap. Mrs Dent rushed out of the kitchen and returned with a green mask strapped across her mouth and her thin body wrapped in a pink overall. She sprayed them both from the industrial spray pack on her back.

'Oh no!' exclaimed Alice. She knew what was coming.

'Go to your room! NOW!' shouted Mr Dent, his voice quivering with fright.

'Here we go again,' Alice muttered. The same thing happened every time she had a cold. And as soon as Alice had gone into her bedroom, Mr Dent locked the specially sealed door so that nothing could escape.

The doctor came to visit that afternoon. She was extremely annoyed to have to come out. She knew the Dents well; Mrs Dent phoned her every day.

'I suspect it's only a virus,' she said crossly, after checking Alice carefully for rashes. 'But I'll have to send this swab for testing; that new Best Minister insists on knowing what germs children have nowadays. Yet more work for me – as if we doctors haven't got enough to do already,' she added, poking a thin stick down Alice's throat. It tickled and before she could stop herself, Alice giggled.

The doctor froze.

'Have you been giggling a lot? Are you feeling cheerful?' she asked suspiciously.

'No, not at all,' said Alice, shaking her head.

'Well don't do it again – don't you know how dangerous it is to giggle right now?' And after another long hard stare at her, the doctor turned to Alice's parents.

'If it's anything more than a common cold, I'll eat my stethoscope.'

'Thank goodness,' said Mrs Dent from behind the door. 'I was afraid that she had the pie Ru—'

'Not in front of the child!' hissed Mr Dent.

'No sign of that, so don't worry. And she can come downstairs – no need for her to stay up here until the results are back; they take days.'

Despite what the doctor had said, Mr and Mrs Dent were taking no chances. Dressed in frilly aprons, green masks and fur-trimmed gloves, they only unlocked Alice's door to deliver foul black medicine on a long-handled spoon or to post chips or toast through the narrow gap. All Alice could do was lie on her bed, getting crosser every day.

'I've got to get out!' she muttered to her Venus flytrap plants. There was a row of these on every windowsill; Mr Dent insisted on it. 'Better than bug spray,' he always declared.

Alice didn't mind them; her room was quite bare otherwise. She kept a few things hidden under a loose floorboard, but Mrs Dent had ruined everything else by putting it through the dishwasher ten times or toasting it in the oven.

Alice was so bored that she ended up talking to the flytraps and feeding them cold chips. After several days, the plants were wilting and Alice was desperate.

'For goodness' sake! You can't lock me up just coz I've got a cold, it's illegal! I'm bored stiff! Please, please, PLEASE let me out!' she pleaded with her parents.

But it was no good.

'No can do, sorry – dangerous things, colds,' said Mr Dent anxiously.

'Especially at your age, it's an unsettled time,' added her mother, posting a cheese triangle through the gap. 'Who knows what might happen?'

'Well I'll die of boredom if you keep me here,' retorted Alice, but her parents had already gone.

By day four, Alice was ready to scream. Her nose was still running, she couldn't help sneezing and she certainly didn't have the giggles the doctor was worried about. In fact she had never been so miserable. Desperate for something to do, Alice had begged for a bath, but Mr Dent wouldn't let her out for anything.

'I can't stand much more of this,' she muttered to the drooping flytraps that evening as she stared aimlessly out of the window on to the dark street below. Nettle Close was unlit at night; Mrs Dent complained daily about the only streetlights being on the main road.

'If only I had a dog,' Alice sighed. But her parents would never let her have pets, not in a million years. Alice wanted a dog most, but she'd settle for anything. (Well, nearly anything – she really didn't think she could cope with a Komodo dragon.)

Just then, her thoughts were interrupted by the

wail of police sirens.

This perked her up a little. There was never trouble on the Chickweed Estate – perhaps for once something exciting might happen. Quickly, Alice turned the light off so she could look out without being spotted.

The noise got closer. Alice held her breath. It sounded like lots of sirens; something serious must be going on.

Abruptly, the sirens stopped mid-wail, very close by. In the sudden hush, Alice heard the low hum of cars turning into Nettle Close.

Staring in disbelief, she watched as five vehicles glided to a halt in front of her house. The cars were very long and very black, and Alice had a feeling that they were very bad news indeed.

Nervous now, she watched the car doors pop open. Then, as all the flashing blue lights and head-lights were switched off, Nettle Close was in darkness again.

Drawing back behind the curtain, Alice listened to the sounds instead. Car doors slamming; the crunch of feet on steam-blasted gravel; a sharp knock on her front door.

There was no response.

'OPEN THIS DOOR NOW OR WE'LL BREAK IT DOWN!'

Alice shivered. *What on earth was going on?*

Then she heard the front door click open.

Peering round the curtain, Alice saw eight large figures standing in the chink of light spilling out from the hall. All wore shiny silver protective suits and masks.

Alice gulped. Four of them were carrying what looked like a battering ram.

That wasn't the worst thing though. What really chilled her blood was that two others carried a long object, big enough to fit a person inside. From the way the light shone through it, it looked transparent.

'Mr Dent?' the voice was official, confident. 'I'm afraid there's a problem.'

'Who are you?' her dad demanded. 'What do you want?'

'We have orders from those in charge. We need to take Alice away.'

What? Alice's stomach flipped over. She couldn't tear her eyes away from the see-through box. It was big enough for a grown-up; they could easily put her inside . . .

'Why? What's wrong with her?' asked Mrs Dent,

leaning out from behind her husband. Alice saw that she had put on gloves, two aprons, two pairs of overshoes, a face visor and a hairnet. Mrs Dent didn't cope well with visitors.

The masked man leant forward, dropping his voice.

Alice strained to listen. Only fragments floated up through the closed window.

'Emergency ... unexpected ... result ... dangerous ... pie ... we need ... pie ... Russ ...'

It was that pie Russ again. But who was Russ? Or maybe they meant pie rust? She was OK then; she hadn't had a pie in weeks. Or maybe they meant the number Pi – but so what?

Her thoughts were going round in circles. Alice concentrated on listening.

'Take her away, right now. She's certainly not staying here, that's for sure,' said Mr Dent, his voice squeaking with fear. 'But you can't come in; you'll utterly ruin the carpets. We'll send her out to you.'

They're going to let them take me! Just like that! Alice was outraged and frightened at the same time. She didn't know what to do.

Then the front door must have fully opened because light streamed out and bounced off the long black cars.

As Alice watched, the beam illuminated the face of a man sitting motionless in the rear seat of the furthest car. His eyes were like black craters, but it was something else that transfixed her. In the slanting light, the man's pale face looked like a flawless wax-like mask.

Surely it can't be him! thought Alice, studying it with increasing horror.

But it was.

And as her legs began to buckle in terror, the new Best Minister for Everything Nicely Perfect lifted his head and looked directly up at her.

CHAPTER TWO
A Very Busy Night

Alice ducked behind the curtain again, heart thudding. Had the Best Minister seen her?

There's no way I'm going to let anyone take me away like that – especially not him! I've got to get out right now!

This thought made Alice feel brave. Very quietly, she slid her feet into her factory-fresh trainers. Then she stuffed her steam-cleaned school bag with a bottle of purified water and slices of stale toast.

17

She was ready to go.

But leaving by the spotlessly scrubbed front door wasn't an option. The only way out was through her bedroom window. Alice sighed. Just her luck that it faced the street where the new Best Minister was waiting. Even worse, everyone else was standing by the porch.

She needed a diversion.

Meanwhile, Mr Dent was still pleading with their visitors.

'Please, if you insist on coming in, take your boots off and go through my super-strength decontamination unit first.'

Alice thought arguing was foolish; the men looked like they meant business.

'Enough! We're coming in! Stand aside!'

'No way! Not without taking your boots off! Hey . . . ARRRGH!'

Alice peered round the curtain. The men had hurled Mr Dent face-first into her mother's favourite plastic rose hedge. Mrs Dent had got it specially made to terrorize next-door's cats – the branches had whisker-snagging fluffy flowers and lethal metal-tipped thorns. Her father would be stuck there for a while.

The men disappeared in through the doorway, slamming the door. As the bright light cut off, the driveway was plunged back into blackness. Alice couldn't see anything. It would be minutes before her eyes adjusted to the dark.

But ... if she couldn't see anything, neither could the Best Minister, still sitting in the car.

It was now or never.

Carefully easing her bedroom window open, she climbed on to the ledge. Below was a big drop to the porch roof. Alice took a deep breath. Despite thinking about jumping out lots of times before, she had never been brave enough. But there was no choice now. She had to get away.

It's too quiet – they'll hear me! Alice fretted. But she needn't have worried, because next-door's cats had found Mr Dent.

'OWWW! Get off my legs, you . . . you . . . mouse-breath vermin! Stop biting me! ARRRGH! Don't you DARE do that on my back ... you ... you ... lousy flea-ridden pests!' he shrieked, struggling uselessly against the thorns.

Alice couldn't help it, she giggled. It was too dark to see what next-door's cats were doing, but she could guess, and she could hear them all right, purring contentedly.

It was the perfect diversion. Hanging by slippery fingertips from the windowsill, Alice waited until Mr Dent let out the loudest scream ever. Then she let go.

THUMP!

Swallowing a yelp, she clung to the porch roof, heart banging.

Had anyone heard?

But the only sound was Mr Dent moaning.

Sliding to the edge of the porch roof, Alice dropped to the side passage and fled into the pink-tiled back garden. Hastily, she scrambled over the garden wall and ran across next-door's medal-winning flower beds, accidently crushing this year's prize dahlias.

She had a horrible feeling that before long there would be a massive search for her, with helicopters and lights. There might even be dogs, big fierce ones with snapping jaws.

But there was no sign of a chase yet and a few gardens later, Alice felt happier. It was great to be outside without being stuffed into a coat. Also she had never been allowed to run across grass or soil before. Mrs Dent always insisted on 'tarmac or concrete only, much more hygienic' and had refused to let Alice go to school on games lesson days in case she trod in something too horrid to think about.

Alice grinned. *I'm free! I can do what I want now!* she thought. Thinking this cheered her up a lot as she jogged on.

But two minutes later, she reached the main road leading out of the estate.

Alice hesitated. The road looked totally exposed in the yellow lamplight – but she knew she had no choice. It was the only exit. Making up her mind, she sprinted forward at top speed, her feet thudding on the hard pavement.

If she could just get off the road before they came looking…

A horrible thought suddenly struck her – *they must know this is the only way out too, that's why they didn't follow me!*

And then Alice heard the low throbbing of a helicopter coming towards her, fast. *Where had that come from?* Horrified, she looked up. The helicopter's searchlight was sweeping down the estate. In a few seconds it would catch her.

She had to get off the road and hide *right now!*

Legs trembling, Alice looked around frantically.

There was a fence on the far side of the road – but it was too high to climb. And the only other option ... Alice looked despairingly at the slanting blackness beside her. It led down to the river.

Going into the water was dangerous.

People drowned doing that. There was no way ...

Then she heard the noise of cars speeding along the main road. Hurriedly, Alice slid down the incline and crouched down by the river bridge.

Below her, inky black water rushed silently past. Above her, sinister black cars swished through the lamplight. The helicopter was getting louder and louder. Alice swallowed and covered her ears, a cold sweat breaking on her skin.

She had got off the road just in time.

The water beside her was foul, with trails of tiny bubbles and the odd plastic bag swirling in the current, but it was her only way out now.

Alice shivered. All she knew about swimming was from reading about it and practising on the carpet. In truth, she'd never swum in anything bigger than the bath. Even though swimming pool water was full of chlorine, her mother never let her go. 'Think of all those nasty diseases you might catch from toddlers with dirty bottoms!' Mrs Dent always said, her eyes full of fear.

As Alice tried frantically to remember how to swim, the whole sky lit up above her. The helicopter was overhead!

That did it. Grabbing a nearby tree branch, she slid nervously into the foul water. *I can hide under the bridge – if I don't drown first!* Alice thought, not believing she was doing this, especially with a cold. She was bound to end up with pneumonia – and Mrs Dent would never forgive her for that.

And then she laughed. She laughed so much with relief that she had to lean against the bridge wall for support.

She didn't need to swim at all – the shallow water barely came up to her knees!

The helicopter hadn't seen her; Alice heard it sweep away, still searching. Quietly, she slipped out into the darkness and waded along in the shallow water.

After that it was easy. Alice scrambled out on to the riverbank footpath just before her stream joined the main river. Soon she had left Nettle Close far behind and was heading out of Knott Sowell town.

The next morning, Alice awoke abruptly from a

nice sleep on an old squishy sofa. She had found it dumped by a bend in the river path, hidden from the road by friendly whispering trees.

Sleeping out under the stars had been fun, but now Alice felt grubby and grumpy and afraid. *I don't know where to go now,* she thought, and that terrified her.

I'm not scared! she told herself fiercely as she ate the stale toast for breakfast.

'I'm not scared!' she said, jumping up and shaking a hopeful pigeon off her lap.

'I'M NOT SCARED!' she shouted, making the timid pigeons around her feet take off in fright. Alice giggled – and giggling made her feel a *lot* better.

'I'M NOT SCARED!' she shouted, even louder.

But as the birds circled overhead, scolding her, Alice froze. She could hear footsteps, the thud of boots along the river path. Heart thudding, Alice dived into the bushes behind the sofa and peered through the leaves.

Had they heard her too?

And as two figures marched around the bend, Alice gulped nervously.

They were police officers.

Both wore bulletproof vests bristling with gadgets. The man was enormous, sweating heavily in his dark-blue uniform. But it was the smaller woman who scared Alice. From her suspicious darting eyes to her eager clawed hands, she was terrifying. Alice cowered lower as they stopped nearby.

'So what's going on here then?' asked the policeman, looking around suspiciously.

The woman lifted her nose and sniffed. 'Those pigeons were spooked by something – there's someone here, Sarge, I can smell them.'

She took a step towards the bush, still sniffing loudly.

Alice could see the woman's boots moving closer. *Oh no!* She was terrified, but strangely she really wanted to giggle . . . she couldn't help it . . . she bit her hand to stop herself . . . she was going to giggle and scream and . . .

Tough bony fingers grabbed her ankle and tugged, hard.

'ARRRGH!' Alice screamed, trembling with fright.

The fingers squeezed tighter.

'Got her!' the policewoman shouted triumphantly, dragging Alice out by her ankle. 'See, told you so!

Right, on your feet, girl and stand to attention!'

'Well, well, what have we here?' the sergeant asked, frowning as Alice scrambled up, trying to stand to attention on wobbly legs.

'And who are you?' he demanded.

Alice didn't know what to say. Telling him her real name was probably not a good idea. But before she could say anything, he abruptly wrinkled his nose and stepped away.

'Eeeh, you *do* smell!'

'No I don't!' Alice protested.

'You do, you know ... and you're covered in dirt,' he said with deep disapproval. 'When did you last wash? Your face is filthy and birds could nest in your hair.'

Alice suddenly remembered her parents talking about the Best Minister's new rules. Her heart filled with dread ... *Oh no! He's getting the police to track down smelly and dirty children*. Of all the rotten luck – why couldn't she have got caught on a day when she'd had at least five showers? She hadn't washed for days, and sleeping on that old sofa was the last straw ...

Her captors exchanged glances.

'A child that doesn't wash ...' said the sergeant

significantly.

'Oh goody, we can use the new Best Minister's latest grimy and grubby children law. I do so love using our brand-new powers.' Smirking widely, the policewoman pulled out a shiny new notebook.

Alice had a very bad feeling about this. Noticing that the notebook cover had a picture of a shield with a clock on it, under what looked like crossed toothbrushes, she really wished she'd listened more to her parents going on about the new Best Minister. Now that she looked, both officers had gleaming badges with the same logo pinned to their vests.

Alice shivered, remembering that face she'd seen in the back of the long black car. Whatever happened, they mustn't find out who she was.

'Make the order for immediate and drastic action. It's for her own good – just look at her hair,' ordered the policeman. He looked at her. 'Now tell me, what's your name, girl?'

Alice hadn't realized how hard it is to make up a pretend name on the spot. She looked around wildly for help.

As the policeman tapped his foot impatiently, a smart blue boat putt-putted past on the river behind him. Its name was painted in bright letters on the bow: Portland Bill.

Well, Bill didn't suit her, but . . .

In desperation, Alice stared at her feet. A small grub was wriggling over one of her dusty shoes.

'Err . . . Portland, my name's Portland, er . . . Portland Maggott.'

'Portland Maggott?' said the policeman in disbelief. 'What kind of a name is that?'

'Mine,' said Alice firmly.

'Hurry up Portland Maggott – get in, girl!'

The policewoman wrenched open the back door of the waiting police car. She shoved Alice inside so hard that Alice ended up sprawled across the back seat.

Unfortunately there was already someone else sitting there.

Mortified, Alice hastily pushed herself upright, off the lap of the scruffy boy staring at her in horror.

'Sorry,' she whispered, her face burning.

'S'all right,' the boy muttered, avoiding her eyes.

Alice slid as far away as possible from him, still flaming with embarrassment as she did up her seat-belt. Turning her back, she looked out of the side window as the two police officers jumped in.

'Right, let's get rid of these two nuisances!' said the policewoman from behind the steering wheel, stamping down on the accelerator. The car leapt forward in a frenzy of flashing lights and wailing sirens.

They travelled at rocket speed, streaking through towns and villages, swerving round corners and through red lights. Alice began to enjoy herself. It was the best car ride she had ever been on. (This was not saying much, as she had never been out of Knott Sowell town before. Her parents panicked at the thought of Alice using public toilets.)

But every mile increased the distance between her and the answers to her questions. She had lots of questions. Why was the Best Minister after her? What was the pie? Who was Russ?

'Hey, is yer name really Portland Maggott?'

Alice turned. The boy was staring at her with curious brown eyes. Alice considered his question. Until she knew what was going on, it was probably better if no one knew her real name.

She nodded.

'Yes – what's yours?'

'Kevin, Kevin Mudd, I'm eleven. Me mum's just been rushed into hospital. The kids have all gone to their dads, but mine couldn't have me, he's in prison,' he told her, scratching his untidy brown hair. There was mud streaked across his face.

'How many brothers and sisters have you got?' asked Alice curiously.

'Six,' replied Kevin, counting them off on his fingers. 'There's Keeley, she's six, then Keith, he's five, Kenny's four, so's Kari-Anne, then little Kiera's two and Klint's the last. He's just a baby, so he went to the hospital with mum.'

He turned away, looking upset. Alice guessed he didn't want to talk about it. She changed the subject quickly.

'Do you know where they're taking us?'

'Some place called Tryton Mell. I heard 'em tell me mum in the ambulance. She was really worried coz it's a long way from here.' Kevin shrugged, scratching his head again. 'Never heard of it so I don't know nothin' else.'

'Never mind, Portland,' called the policeman from the passenger seat. 'We'll track down your parents, no doubt about that. Then we'll slap them with the Best Minister's new thing for grown-ups who don't look after children properly: the Shiny and Sparkling Children's Order. They can pick you up after they've done the compulsory training and you've all had a good scrub. Meanwhile, you're off to Tryton Mell School. Gertriss Grammaticus, the headmistress, is excellent at sorting out grimy children like you two.'

He turned to smile at her. 'Soon your worries will be over.'

Only if you don't find out who I really am, thought Alice.

Hours later the car swerved off the road and halted in front of a pair of gigantic gates. Not just any old gates, these were fortified top-of-the-range castle gates – every inch of nailed wood polished to dazzling brilliance. Large letters were carved into the archway above:

TRYTON MELL

'Here we are!' trilled the policewoman happily, as the gates swung open.

The narrow drive behind the gates twisted through a storybook forest. Some trees were perfect for climbing; others curled into ready-made dens.

But Alice noticed that all overhanging branches along the driveway had been brutally cut. The freshly scarred trees were now exactly in line with the tarmac edge. Not a single leaf or twig blighted the pristine road. It didn't look quite right somehow.

'Too neat, gives me a rash,' muttered Kevin. Alice thought it was a good thing he hadn't visited her house – it would probably give him boils.

But they had an even greater shock when the car drew up in front of the house.

'Frazzling Fruitcakes!' said Kevin faintly.

Alice couldn't speak.

House was the wrong word. It looked like someone had taken a handful of mansions, thrown in a couple of castles, stirred in a few farm buildings then added a few parks for good measure.

'What a weird place!' Alice managed to say at last, but Kevin seemed too overwhelmed to reply.

They scrambled out of the car as the policeman tugged the gleaming bell pull beside the massive front door. While they waited, Alice and Kevin studied the dazzlingly bright blue plastic sign by the side of the door.

Tryton Mell
Turning grubby good-for-nothings
into politely perfect pupils

They exchanged alarmed glances.

'I don't like the sound of that,' whispered Alice, her heart sinking.

'It's really loose – look, there's something underneath,' said Kevin. He twisted the plaque. Underneath was another plaque – this one looked old, made of weathered brass. In friendly round letters it said:

Welcome to Tryton Mell
Professor Tryton says
'Have fun every day the Tryton way'

'They've rebranded,' the policeman explained, noticing what Kevin was doing. 'Now put that back at once!'

'I liked their old brand better,' muttered Kevin. He dropped the plaque hastily as they heard the click of a lock turning.

The perfectly varnished door began to open, soundless on well-oiled hinges.

'Oh no!' Alice reeled backwards as she caught sight of the person on the doorstep.

CHAPTER THREE
The Head of Dusting and Discipline

lice couldn't believe it.

The glaring woman at the door looked exactly like a giant version of Mrs Dent.

Admittedly, this was mostly because she was pointing a supersize spray gun directly at them, but it didn't help that she was also wearing a dazzling white apron, gloves and rubber boots.

'DUCK!' shouted Kevin, but it was too late. The woman soaked them both with flower-scented spray before they could move.

'HEY – watch it! Them's me best trainers!' shrieked Kevin.

'That's just great!' muttered Alice crossly, shaking disinfectant out of her hair.

'Hello Mrs Peasley!' said the policeman, smiling. He had jumped neatly out of the way.

Mrs Peasley ignored him. She was too busy frowning at Kevin and Alice.

'Not *more* children, surely? I don't know where you lot find them all.'

She peered at Kevin.

'And *another* boy? He's bound to have nits. Looks like a troublemaker too. I hope he's less bother than the last one you fetched in.'

She gave Alice a hard stare. 'And a girl, we're not keen on girls, sly things, always falling out with each other. Look at the state of this one, really filthy – and smelly. Nothing nice about her at all.'

Alice flushed. People at school were always saying nasty things to her about her parents, but she'd never been called smelly before.

Beside her, Kevin had gone rigid. He glared at Mrs Peasley.

'Yer not a great looker yerself are yer?'

The silence that followed was very long. Mrs Peasley swelled up, her face changing from white to red to purple.

Alice watched with breathless interest, almost choking on a giggle. Mrs Peasley looked like she was going to explode.

'How DARE you . . . you . . . RUDE . . . you'll be sorry! You wait till . . .'

The policeman coughed loudly.

'Well, I'll best be off now,' he said, shooting Mrs Peasley a warning glance. 'Do *try* and keep these children alive until I've left – I can't face any more paperwork today.'

This made Mrs Peasley glare at Alice and Kevin even more fiercely, but she kept her mouth clamped shut until the police car had disappeared down the drive.

Then she spoke.

'Not a step further until you numpkins have put these on!' she said crossly, throwing them both fluffy bundles of blue and pink fuzz.

'What are they?' asked Alice, puzzled. The bundles looked remarkably like mutant rabbits.

'Polishing socks of course!' Mrs Peasley snapped. 'You can wear them until I've fitted you for regulation school shoes. Now get on with it – I haven't got all day!'

As Alice and Kevin hurriedly slipped off their trainers, Mrs Peasley sealed her nostrils with a giant clothes peg and grabbed their shoes with thick metal tongs. Shuddering, she dropped each item into a bright yellow bin.

'Oi, they're really expensive trainers!'

'Tough, they're contaminated waste now. Right, follow me!'

'She'd better give me them trainers back or mum will go spare!' muttered Kevin mutinously.

Mrs Peasley pretended not to hear him, but a nasty little smile broke over her face as she led them through the doorway into the entrance hall beyond.

'It's ginormous!' whispered Kevin.

Alice stared around in disbelief. The colossal hall was the most amazing room she'd ever seen. The burnished wood of the wall panels glowed gold under a waterfall of lamps. Light reflected from every sparkling surface; even the grey stone floor looked as squeaky bright as a dishwasher-blasted plate and was as slippery as an ice rink.

'It's all so . . . so . . . polished!' she couldn't

help exclaiming.

'Of course it is!' Mrs Peasley retorted, looking smug.

But it wasn't just the sheer size of the hall, or the dazzling cleanliness – it wasn't even the over-whelming smell of disinfectant that got them. It was also the fact that everything was a little odd.

The fireplace that faced them was normal enough, except that it was so massive that Santa Claus, his sleigh and entire team of reindeer could have performed stunts in it. But the old-fashioned red telephone box looked out of place, and there was a real live tree growing through one corner of the room.

A forest of swings hung down from its stout branches, but all were chained up and secured with a shiny padlock and chain. Next to it was a round-about and two seesaws, all chained up too.

And everything, even the statues, an umbrella stand, three gigantic clocks and the tree (leaves and all) was covered in sheets of clear plastic.

'What's with the plastic?' Kevin muttered, skat-ing expertly along in his fluffy socks.

'Well, I suppose it's easy to wipe clean,' suggested Alice. (Mrs Dent loved plastic sheeting. Nothing cheered her up more than unfolding a new wipe-clean cover and laying it down over a freshly vacuumed carpet.)

Kevin stared at her in disgust.

'What *is* this place?' he asked plaintively – and far too loudly.

Mrs Peasley halted at once, spinning on her heels to face them.

'That's enough talking, numbskulls!' she snarled. 'Now shut up and listen to me, you grimy good-for-nothings! You want to know what Tryton Mell is? Well, I'll tell you – it's a place for horrid dirty children like you two. First we're going to scrub you clean and get rid of any nasty little critters you're carrying. Next we'll drill you until you lose all those terrible do-what-you-like habits that you picked up from your lazy mums or dads or other useless grown-ups. Then we'll work on turning you into polite, rule-abiding little robots. Finally, if you're lucky and live that long, we'll teach you to shine and sparkle.'

Alice could see Kevin's look of absolute horror. She wasn't feeling too good about it herself.

'I don't want to sparkle!' Kevin protested.

'Sparkling's compulsory,' said Mrs Peasley severely.

'How long do we have to stay here?'

'Oh, probably for ever. No child's left yet, no one's ever passed the leaving exam.'

'But . . . the police said . . . my mum could come . . .'

'That's just to keep parents quiet, for some reason they always get upset when you take their precious little brats away. Mind you, once they've been without them for a few months and their house stops smelling and stays clean and tidy, they never seem to want them back.'

Kevin had gone quite white by this time. This seemed to satisfy Mrs Peasley. She pointed behind them.

'Now read the rules. Make sure you memorize them, we test you on them twice a day. And be warned, numpties, if you break any of these rules, you'll be lucky to survive your punishment.'

'This ain't gonna be good,' muttered Kevin as they both turned to see where she was pointing.

Hung from the rafters in the centre of the hall was a ten metre high wooden noticeboard. Bold black words were carved into the gleaming wood. With a feeling of doom, Alice lifted her eyes to the title:

TRYTON MELL SCHOOL RULES

'Stay here and DON'T touch anything while I fetch your lovely uniforms!' ordered Mrs Peasley sternly. With that, she disappeared behind one of the many polished wooden doors that lined the walls.

'I really don't think I'm gonna like it here,' muttered Kevin.

And as Alice studied the first few rules with a rapidly sinking heart, she could only agree with him.

1. <u>No</u> giggling (or smiling or laughing or having fun) at <u>any</u> time.

2. Coughing or sneezing or snotty noses will <u>not</u> be tolerated. Pupils with any nasty illness symptoms must report to the school nurse <u>immediately</u>.

3. Hands and nails must be clean and shiny at <u>all</u> times.

4. Teachers are <u>always</u> right.

5. Pupils must be silent at <u>all</u> times.

6. Pupils must not be more than ten seconds early or late for <u>anything</u>.

7. Anyone talking about Professor Tryton (or the fun times they had when he was headmaster) will be <u>severely</u> punished.

There were 253 rules listed in total, but Alice really didn't want to read any more.

'What rubbish rules!' muttered Kevin. 'I can't go a day without having a laugh!'

He thinks he's got problems? thought Alice, stifling a cough. *I'm already breaking the second rule!* She had a horrible feeling about the giggling rule too. Now she thought about it, she'd felt giggly on and off all morning.

'Forget them rules for now – look right up there!' Kevin pointed upwards.

Alice looked up. Tiers of balconies ran around the walls, each reached by curving staircases. Oddly, the stairs were flanked by what looked like wooden slides.

'They can't be slides!' Alice was disbelieving.

'Don't be stupid, girl, of course they are!'

Mrs Peasley had returned, carrying a neat pile of brown clothes. 'Sliding's compulsory here for going downstairs. We can't have grimy little children holding handrails with the same unwashed hands that have just wiped dirty little bottoms. That would spread nasty germs.'

Kevin frowned. 'But how do we go upstairs?'

'Don't be an idiot, boy – have some common

sense! You use the stairs of course, but no touching the rails, you put your hands behind your back. We tried that going downstairs as well but children have no sense of balance. They would keep falling and breaking things. Right, that's enough of this time-wasting. Follow me – let's get you nincompoops kitted out before Miss Grammaticus sees you, or you'll be doing punishment chores for the rest of your lives.'

Mrs Peasley's spotlessly scrubbed office was behind one of the mysterious doors leading off in all directions from the hall. Alice read the nameplate:

Mrs Feather Peasley
Head of Discipline and Dusting

'I'd never have guessed,' muttered Kevin, rolling his eyes as they entered. Unfortunately this made him walk straight into a large silver feather-topped trophy, which made Alice want to giggle quite badly.

'Don't touch my champion dusting award!' screamed Mrs Peasley, grabbing Kevin's ear and towing him furiously through her office.

Behind her, a little red printer labelled 'Red Alerts' gave a cheerful belch.

'Brrrr . . . up!' it chirruped, spitting out two sheets of scarlet-tinged paper just as Alice passed. And as she glanced down, her giggles vanished immediately.

Splashed across the top of the first sheet, in jaw-breakingly large letters, was her name:

ALICE DENT

And underneath was a picture – a full colour photo of herself that she recognized at once.

Cold with shock, Alice looked around. Mrs Peasley had grabbed an enormous pump labelled 'MOUSE 'N' LOUSE KILL' and was pinning a frantically struggling Kevin to the floor with one foot. Lingering behind as Kevin disappeared, protesting in a cloud of white powder, Alice hastily stuffed both pages of the Red Alert into her pocket.

Ten minutes later, Alice stood next to Kevin in front of a shiny mirror and stared at her new uniform.

'It's very brown,' she said doubtfully.

'Such a lovely practical colour,' mused Mrs Peasley.

The uniform was incredibly well ironed. Each crease in Alice's brown tunic was so sharp that it could slice through butter. Everything was edged with crimson trim, even their shirts had smart red and white stripes.

'I hate wearing tights,' she whispered to Kevin. It didn't help that she had stuffed the Red Alert down them in the changing cubicle.

'Nothing worse than brown trousers,' replied Kevin gloomily.

'Blazers on!' instructed Mrs Peasley. 'Full school uniform must be worn at all times.'

'What about weekends?' asked Alice.

'You wear full uniform at all times.'

'What – even in bed?'

'Don't be stupid, boy!' Mrs Peasley said severely, grabbing Kevin's tie and knotting it tighter.

'Oww! Too tight!'

Alice hastily adjusted her own tie. She had to admit that it was very smart, all gold emblems on a crimson background . . .

Prickling with horror, she looked more closely. She had seen that shield emblem before. A clock under what looked like crossed toothbrushes – the same symbol that was on the shiny badges the police had worn.

It was on her blazer too. Alice's hands trembled. *If the Best Minister is linked to Tryton Mell and they find out who I really am, I'm doomed!* she thought.

'You look like proper little school children now,' Mrs Peasley grinned. 'Right, hand over your phones – you're not allowed them here.'

'Got none!'

But even Alice could tell that Kevin was fibbing.

Mrs Peasley laughed.

Her laugh was far worse than her grin. She sounded like the mad woman in all the worst horror films. Alice began to shudder and even Kevin looked scared.

'Give it to me, you little liar!'

'No!' Kevin was defiant. 'Mum might want me; she's really poorly and—'

'You can use the phone in the hall, it's regularly disinfected.'

'No blinking way!'

'Oh excellent, a snotty little refuser – I get to use my electronic device detector. CUDDLES! Come to Mummy!'

There was a white flash. A gigantic toddler-sized furry object burst into the chamber and hopped over to them.

'A rabbit?' Kevin laughed incredulously. 'I'm not scared.'

Mrs Peasley bristled. 'You should be. That's not just any old rabbit, that's a lethal weapon which is also completely housetrained. Find, Cuddles!'

The overgrown white rabbit hopped over to Kevin and leapt forward.

'Ooohhh!' Kevin fell backwards.

'I c-can't b-breathe!' he groaned as Cuddles sat triumphantly on his chest, pawing at his blazer pocket. Smirking, Mrs Peasley extracted Kevin's phone and slipped it smugly into her own pocket, throwing Cuddles a carrot as a reward.

'NOOOOO! Give it back!' Kevin howled.

'Stop that dreadful noise at once and come with me – it's dinner time!' Crossly, Mrs Peasley pushed Kevin forward.

But Alice lingered, watching the rabbit. He didn't eat the carrot. Instead he came and sat on Alice's feet, gazing up at her adoringly.

'Shoo! Go away!' Alice hissed, but he wouldn't move. Strangely alarmed by this, Alice hastily extracted her feet and dashed off after the others.

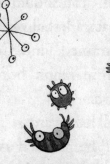

CHAPTER FOUR
The Food with No Smell

Mrs Peasley led them down a wide passageway, humming happily as she flicked her duster over the gleaming walls.

'I'm an amazing duster, you know,' she told them proudly. 'I've been world champion twenty-seven times in a row.'

'Don't see the point of dusting,' Kevin replied. 'It always comes back again.'

Mrs Peasley turned purple. Alice really thought

she would explode this time. Instead the teacher prodded Kevin hard with the duster handle all the way along the main corridor.

There were smaller passages leading off from this, but each one was sealed with a solid steel grille, an enormous golden padlock and planks nailed over and over in a frenzy of woodwork.

Someone was making very sure indeed that all the side passages stayed closed.

Alice thought this was a real shame because each sealed-off passage was marked by an intriguing looking signpost.

She spotted 'The Windy Gap', 'The Passage of Doom', 'The Bog' and one she quite fancied called 'Walk of the Stars'.

'Do yer reckon them blocked corridors are left over from when that Professor Tryton was in charge?' whispered Kevin excitedly.

Alice nodded – she thought this too.

One called 'Short Cut Bounce' caught her eye. Cautiously, she veered over to get a closer look, peeping through a hole in a plank. To her surprise, the floor was entirely made of trampoline, invitingly stretching into the distance.

'Come away!' screeched Mrs Peasley, grabbing

Alice's arm.

'Is it really trampoline?' Kevin asked, bubbling with curiosity.

'SILENCE!'

Kevin pulled a face behind Mrs Peasley's back. Alice hastily looked away, frantically swallowing a giggle.

'Here's the dining hall,' said Mrs Peasley, glaring at them as she stopped beside a pair of double doors, all shiny wood and black-studded nails.

'I hope the food's OK,' Kevin whispered, as Mrs Peasley shoved them forward, then turned and marched huffily back along the corridor.

They both stood nervously in the doorway and stared into the dining hall.

'Looks like a blinking mud bath,' muttered Kevin.

Alice knew what he meant. There were hundreds of pupils sitting at the long tables, all wearing neat brown uniforms. The overwhelming brownness was broken only by the dazzling stripes of their school shirts and the snowy tablecloths glowing under moon-like lamps. As the pupils ate, light reflected in blinding flashes from polished knives and sparkling glasses.

But what struck Alice most was the silence. All she could hear was the scrape of plates and clink of cutlery.

'It's proper dinner,' Kevin whispered, sounding disgusted. 'I wanted chips.'

Strangely there was no smell of food, but it looked OK. Alice could see silver serving dishes piled high with potatoes, vegetables and roast meat.

'Too many vegetables,' muttered Kevin, gloomier by the second. Alice didn't care. She was starving; her stale-toast breakfast was a very long time ago.

'More troublesome new arrivals to bother me, I see. Names? Ages? Quickly now!'

The man who appeared in front of them had a long black dinner jacket, a perfectly tied bow tie and a seriously bad attitude.

'Names? Ages?' he repeated impatiently.

'Err . . . me name's Mudd – Kevin Mudd.'

'Al . . . Portland Maggott.' Alice only just remembered in time. 'We're both eleven.'

'Are yer a dinner lady?' asked Kevin curiously.

They both recoiled at the man's expression.

'I'm Mr Ricard – Master of the Dining Hall,' the man said frostily. 'But you will call me "sir".'

And after that, things got rapidly worse. Mr

Ricard swivelled to face the pupils.

'MR KEVIN MUDD AND MISS PORTLAND MAGGOTT!' he announced, his voice shaking the plates. Everyone immediately turned to stare at them. Alice was so embarrassed that she wanted the floor to swallow her up, but beside her Kevin smiled and waved like royalty.

The room seemed crammed full of pupils. As Mr Ricard marched them down the hall, Alice noticed that at every table the boys sat facing the girls.

'Sit there!' Mr Ricard ordered, pointing to the only table with spaces.

Thankful to escape the staring, Alice slid on to the wooden bench. Eagerly she reached out for the nearest serving dish.

'Wait!' whispered the girl beside her, grabbing Alice's sleeve.

'Trugg! Service!' ordered Mr Ricard, snapping his fingers. He frowned at Alice's neighbour. 'No talking, Merrikin – no excuses, you know the rules.' He bent and banged the table with his fist, making plates and pupils jump.

'And finish your food girl, you know what happens if you leave anything on your plate.'

Alice felt the girl beside her shudder.

'Ah . . . Trugg, you're here. Excellent, main courses for these two.'

Alice stared at Trugg. He was tall, good-looking, slightly older than her and dressed in the smartest school uniform she had ever seen. It was all razor-sharp creases, but with shiny gold trim instead of crimson like hers.

But the way Trugg looked at her and Kevin when Mr Ricard walked away made Alice's heart squeeze. She'd met enough school bullies to know that look very well indeed.

Trugg studied them as he pulled on white gloves. Alice looked hastily away, wondering if the gold trim on his uniform meant that he was a prefect. If so, she and Kevin were already in trouble.

'Go easy on the veg, mate!' called Kevin.

Everyone gasped.

Trugg looked at Kevin, smiling as he piled on spoonful after spoonful of vegetables from every serving dish on to the plate.

Kevin opened his mouth. Alice saw the black-haired boy opposite her urgently shake his head at him.

Trugg banged the piled up plate down in front of Kevin.

'You'll eat what you're given and like it, Mudd.'

He turned to Alice. 'Any requests from you, Maggott-face?'

Alice shook her head. She looked down until Trugg slammed her plate in front of her and walked away. It too had an awful lot of vegetables on it.

'You're lucky you missed the first three courses,' whispered the girl beside her as Trugg strode away. She had long red-brown hair pulled back into neat plaits, dark eyes and a quick nervous smile.

'I'm Chloe, Chloe Merrikin, and he's Jago Smiley.' Chloe nodded to the unsmiling black-haired boy opposite. Alice thought Mrs Peasley's plan was working well on Jago. He looked a bit like a robot, with a flawless face and hair so neat it looked like it had been painted on. She couldn't imagine a more unsuitable surname for him.

'Have you had your injection against measles?' Jago asked abruptly.

'What?'

'Jago, shut up!' Chloe frowned at him. 'Sorry, he's got a thing about that; he won't sit with anyone who's not up to date with all their jabs, especially against measles and things.'

'Oh don't worry, I've had everything.' (This was

true – Mr Dent used to drop Alice off at the doctor's, with a note around her neck demanding that Alice get all the latest vaccines. The doctor's receptionist kept a special chair for Alice and fed her sherbet lollies.)

'Yeah, and I'm all done,' Kevin told Jago. 'Me mum made sure of that.'

'Good,' said Jago, still not smiling. Alice thought he would have no trouble with the no giggling or laughing rule.

Chloe smiled instead. 'Sorry I grabbed you – but you get punished if you help yourself here.'

'That's OK,' said Alice, giving up trying to decide which of the seven forks to use. Choosing the smallest one, she speared a piece of carrot and popped it into her mouth.

'What the—!'

The carrot was hard and icy cold, burning her mouth. Alice spat it out.

'All the food's cooked for hours then frozen,' explained Chloe, suppressing a nervous smile. 'Stops bugs growing on it. Miss Grammaticus the headmistress hates germs.'

'So does my mum,' said Alice grimly. At least Mrs Dent had never thought about serving all their food frozen. Alice was going to make very sure that her mum and this Miss Grammaticus never met.

'What – everything's *frozen*?' asked Kevin, snapping out of his misery.

'Yeah, everything,' said Chloe, nodding. 'Well, this month, anyway. Last month we had to barbecue everything at the table until it was charred, to sterilize it.'

'Yeah, that was fun!' the boy next to Jago smiled at the memory. 'Trouble was we kept setting fire to tablecloths and eyebrows and things so the fire service banned it.'

There was a sudden noise at the other end of the hall. Two pupils seemed to have collapsed. Mr Ricard strode towards them with a pile of blankets.

'Hypothermia,' Chloe explained, seeing Alice stare. 'The little kids eat too quickly and the cold makes them pass out.'

'Isn't that really dangerous?' Alice was shocked.

'Yeah, but Miss Grammaticus worries about germs more.'

'What about gravy – is that frozen as well?' asked Alice. Gravy would help with eating peas. She hated peas.

Using a clean knife, Jago pushed the gravy jug

over to Alice. She looked inside. The gravy was frozen into a slushy lump.

'Look on the bright side, it stops you making a mess on the tablecloth,' said Chloe.

Kevin was now tucking into his plate of frozen vegetables.

'Bit like eating ice – can't taste nothing,' he said happily.

'Shovel it in quick,' advised the cheerful looking boy next to Jago. 'It's worse thawed.' Alice liked the look of him immediately; he had wavy straw-coloured hair and the biggest grin she had ever seen.

'Shhh Oscar!' Jago whispered anxiously. 'Shut up all of you! You're breaking the rules!'

And at this warning everyone nervously clamped their mouths shut.

By the time Alice had reached the frozen sponge pudding and iced custard course she never wanted to eat ice cream again.

'Doesn't all this ice crack your teeth?' she wondered, forgetting to whisper.

'Shhh!' Jago hissed urgently, but it was too late.

'Breaking the silence rule already, Maggott?' Trugg loomed over her, his eyes gleaming.

'Leave her alone Trugg,' said Jago quietly. 'She's

only just arrived.'

Alice gazed at Jago in surprise. He'd been so unfriendly ever since she'd sat down, but now here he was standing up to Trugg.

'That's not—' Trugg broke off, turning, his hand dropping.

Alice felt it too, a ripple running through the silent dining hall, the silence solidifying into fear.

The doors at the far end had opened.

Everybody in the hall scrambled to their feet and stood behind their benches. Alice and Kevin hastily copied them. Trugg melted away to his table as a tall thin lady, dressed entirely in elegant black, glided in through the doors. Apart from her pale face, everything about her was black: her hair, her long nails and the sleek coat of the enormous hound at her heels.

'What sort of dog is *that*?' Kevin asked.

'Mutant man-eater,' Oscar told him gloomily.

'MISS GRAMMATICUS!' announced Mr Ricard.

It was as if the room had been dipped in freezing solution. Alice shivered, half expecting to see a crazy paving of frost racing across the floor towards her.

'Don't look up!' whispered Chloe. Alice noticed that everyone was staring at the floor.

'And watch out for Precious,' Chloe nodded towards the dog. 'He's really mean. He's there to stop anyone getting too close to Miss Grammaticus. She doesn't like being touched.'

'You horrible hornets!' said Miss Grammaticus, her voice icicle-sharp. 'I've heard reports of disgraceful behaviour today. Mr Ricard, read out the naughty list.'

Mr Ricard unrolled a long scroll of paper. Alice felt everyone around her go tense. It was obviously very bad news to be on the list.

'Daniel Duck – filthy bathroom habits.

'Donna Davies – disgusting girl's picking her nose again.'

The whole room groaned. Alice guessed that Donna was always in trouble for this.

'SILENCE!' roared Miss Grammaticus. 'Do carry on, Mr Ricard – ignore these bad-mannered delinquents.'

'Maisie Evans – giggling in maths.

'Billy Frugal – dirty boy's been wiping his nose on his sleeve.'

As each name was called a white-faced pupil left their place and lined up neatly in front of Miss Grammaticus.

'Nita Patel – horrible nasty rash on arms.'

'That's not her fault,' whispered Kevin. 'How can she help that?'

'Zuzanna Piotrowska – verrucas.'

'Quincy Quick – telling jokes.'

As the list went on, Alice badly wanted to giggle. She was beginning to feel curiously happy. That made no sense; she should be feeling more miserable than ever. She gulped hard. It would be madness to make any noise now.

Unfortunately at that moment, without warning, she sneezed instead.

It was only a very quiet sneeze but . . .

Every sound stopped.

Alice heard Chloe groan. She didn't dare look up. She could feel a chill moving closer. Precious growled menacingly.

'Who sneezed?' Miss Grammaticus was by their table now. 'Precious – grab the culprit!'

Alice froze, terrified, but it was no good.

All teeth bared and snarling, Precious halted in front of her, nose quivering as he sniffed her suspiciously all over.

I'm dead! thought Alice in horror, hastily squeezing her eyes tightly shut.

But then something very odd happened.

Precious stopped snarling.

Cautiously, Alice opened one eye. He was still there, staring intently up at her.

'Precious – COME HERE!' thundered Miss Grammaticus, but Precious ignored her.

Please go away! Alice silently begged him, terrified. And just as if he understood, Precious turned and padded smoothly back to Miss Grammaticus.

Rigid with rage, the headmistress grabbed Precious's collar and towed him out of the hall, the naughty-list pupils trailing unhappily after her.

'What was all that about?' asked Oscar, looking puzzled, but Alice couldn't tell him.

'Whatever you do, Portland, don't be infectious!' warned Chloe as Alice stifled another sneeze. 'Miss Grammaticus will lock you up and throw away the key. Poor Michaela Pink's been locked up since she had chickenpox and that was three months ago!'

'What happens if you're on the list?' Kevin asked Chloe.

'Four hours of punishment circuits. It's drain dipping and sewer scrubbing today.'

'At least it's not The Cage,' said Oscar.

Alice rubbed her nose. There was no way she was going to be locked up; she'd had enough of that at home. If only her cold would go. Whatever she did, she had to hide it.

CHAPTER FIVE
A Most Extraordinary Bath

Clearing up after dinner took ages. As she stacked plates, Alice wondered what was going on back at her house in Nettle Close. Were her parents sorry that she had disappeared, or as glad as she was about it? Would the Best Minister find her here? And how long could she pretend to be Portland Maggott before someone found out who she really was?

'Do we have to do this every meal?' Kevin asked, expertly juggling cutlery.

'Quiet!' warned Jago sharply.

The silence that followed this was broken by an orange slush-ball. It whizzed through the air and landed on the table.

'What the—?' Kevin poked it with a fork.

'STOP THAT AT ONCE!' ordered Mr Ricard, sprinting to the far end of the hall.

'It's the Dunces; they never learn,' said Chloe.

'Yeah – only have a slush-ball fight if you're not going to get caught,' grinned Oscar. 'Shame coz it's perfect colour-coded ammunition, one side milk slush, the other orange slush. We've had some great battles – and great bruises.' A dreamy far-away look came into his eyes.

Chloe looked disapproving.

'Are you ever going to grow up?'

'Will we be in the same class as you?' Alice asked Chloe, hastily changing the subject. Mr Ricard was busy at the other end; it seemed safe to talk.

'Probably not. It depends how far away Miss Grammaticus thinks you are from being perfect. She decides on everyone's group. Each year's split into four sets. There's the Dire Dunces, the Almost Acceptable Averages—'

'That's us,' interrupted Oscar cheerfully.

'That's us,' agreed Chloe, pointing to the silver 'A' badge on her blazer. 'Next there's the Clean and Clevers. There are only two of them – none in our year – then there's the Gleaming Geniuses. There's only one Gleaming Genius in the whole school and that's Jago.'

'Jago?' said Kevin, sounding astonished.

'Yeah, he's in our year too. Groups are separated for most lessons but the C and Cs and Jago join the Averages for things like meals and dormitories.'

'But we never mix with the Dunces,' said Oscar.

'Almost never,' Chloe agreed. 'There's so many of them anyway; there's a lot less of us.'

If Jago's the only Genius, which set is Trugg in?' Alice asked curiously.

'None of them,' said Chloe darkly. 'Miss Grammaticus thinks Harvester Trugg's already perfect. He's one of the four Perfect Poppets.'

'Perfect Poppets?' Kevin rolled his eyes.

'Yeah, it's what Miss Grammaticus calls her favourite pupils. They get to do what they want.'

'Are they prefects?'

'Pretty much. The teachers use 'em to do their dirty work.'

'How do you get to be a Perfect Poppet?' Alice

was curious.

'Spend hours in front of the mirror so you always look perfect, be really nasty and never do anything wrong,' said Chloe bitterly.

'Nah, don't listen to her, she's making that up,' Oscar told them. 'The truth is that their parents are Miss Grammaticus's friends so they're just born horrible.'

'Seriously – she's got *friends*?' Kevin looked incredulous.

'Hope we're Average,' Alice muttered to him as they stacked plates. She had a horrible feeling that Miss Grammaticus would put new arrivals in the Dunces' group.

Kevin shook his head gloomily.

'It's not blooming likely, is it?'

The dormitories were spread over two floors. The boys were on the lower floor, the girls above.

'See yer tomorrow, Portland,' whispered Kevin, as the girls filed upstairs behind Mrs Peasley, each dormitory group peeling off neatly as they arrived at their door.

Chloe seemed nice, but Alice didn't like leaving Kevin. *I hope we're in the same set tomorrow,* she thought anxiously.

Mrs Peasley eyed her with distaste.

'Portland Maggott, you're such a nuisance; now I've got to find you a bed.'

'Perhaps she could sleep in our dormitory tonight, Mrs Peasley. Michaela Pink's bed is still empty,' suggested Chloe helpfully.

Alice held her breath.

'Hmmm, I suppose that will do. Maggott, follow Merrikin.'

And as Chloe turned off to her dormitory, she pulled a relieved Alice in with her.

'Great! You're with us! I wasn't sure Mrs Peasley would go for it, but she did.'

'She hates me,' said Alice with certainty.

'Don't worry, she hates everyone.'

Alice looked around. The dormitory could have been really nice but someone had worked very hard to make it miserable. The walls and floors were gravy coloured and there were long brown curtains over the high windows. A double row of washbasins ran along the middle of the room.

'How many of us sleep here?' asked Alice, looking at the metal framed beds lining the two long walls. The beds were squeezed tightly together, each separated by brown bed curtains, with barely enough room for the tiny wardrobes in between.

'Twenty-eight,' replied Chloe. 'Miss Grammaticus likes to pack us in tightly; she can get more kids in the school then.'

The bedspreads were the same colour and material as the uniforms and curtains. Alice picked hers up in disbelief. 'Does Miss Grammaticus own the company that makes this material or something?' she muttered.

The older-looking girl sitting on the next bed looked up and smiled.

'Hi, I'm Emerald, Emerald Baker,' she said, brushing a mass of ginger curls.

'Hi!' said Alice. 'I'm Al . . . Portland Maggott.'

Emerald stared. 'Wow, I did hear right at dinner! I thought Emerald was bad enough, and I was only saddled with it coz I had green eyes, but Portland! You poor kid!' She expertly twisted her hair into two perfect plaits.

Alice ignored this.

'What's that?' she asked, pointing to something that looked like a badly made sculpture.

'That's the old hot chocolate tap,' said Emerald. 'Professor Tryton's invention. It doesn't work now.'

'By the way, we're not supposed to talk in the

dorms,' warned Chloe.

'It's all right,' said Emerald, grinning, 'coz I'm dormitory head and I say it's OK.'

'Just make sure you don't get caught,' said Chloe darkly as Alice opened the door of her tiny wardrobe. There was nothing much inside apart from a toothbrush, toothpaste and a bottle of green liquid soap. Alice wondered how she was going to wash her hair. Reaching into the back, she found a pile of shapeless brown folds.

'What on earth's this?'

Chloe turned to look. 'Oh, that's your bathsuit.'

'My what?'

'Bathsuit.'

As Alice stared at her, bewildered, a mournful clang echoed through the dormitory.

'It's bath time now. Look, I'll show you . . . put it on.'

Alice pulled the bed curtains. Around her the others were doing the same. But as she undressed, something fell to the floor.

It was the Red Alert she'd taken from Mrs Peasley's office.

Alice's heart skipped a beat. So much had happened that she had forgotten about it. Snatching up the pages, she sat down on the hard bed and read it at last.

The words on the first sheet were in bold black ink.

ALICE DENT
This girl is DEADLY and highly DANGEROUS.
If seen DO NOT APPROACH.
ANY sightings MUST be reported.

Alice's stomach plummeted. She couldn't breathe. But even worse, underneath her name was her last school photo.

Alice hated that picture. It was the worst one ever. The day before, Mr Dent had frazzled her hair by using extra-concentrated nit killer. She looked like a distressed poodle in a blue checked dress; her class had laughed for a whole week after they had seen it. Yet now Alice was glad the picture was so bad. Surely no one could recognize her from that – not in Tryton Mell uniform with her hair so neatly plaited.

'Hurry up everyone!' shouted Emerald. She shook Alice's curtain. 'You OK Portland?'

'F-f-fine . . . just a minute . . .'

Shaking, Alice picked up the second sheet. This was a handwritten note, marked 'FOR THE URGENT ATTENTION OF MISS

GRAMMATICUS.' Alice knew you should never read someone else's mail but this was an emergency.

Dear Miss Grammaticus,

I hope you're getting all those grubby good-for-nothing children scrubbed and better behaved. The police have instructions to send you as many as possible; every child in the country would benefit from being under your care.

I'm sending you this letter to warn you that the Dent child might come your way. I nearly had her, but she's cleverer than she looks and slipped past my men. They've been severely punished, but that doesn't help us to find her. This is a disaster — it's been confirmed that she's got a Pirus...

Alice gulped, trying not to panic. There it was in black and white: Pirus. *Not a Pie Russ then.* But what on earth was a Pirus?

She read on.

...luckily her doctor followed my instructions to check out all snotty children just in case and swabbed her throat so we picked it up.

You know what will happen if it spreads. We might be safe though, my men have been searching for any trace of the Pirus antidote since the

Dent child was detected and we know now that there's one vial left. We just need to find it.

Meanwhile, I've ordered all public health doctors and nurses to stand by; we might have to quarantine whole schools full of children by the time we find the little wretch. We know that if one child catches it, they'll all get it; they're such nasty little super-spreaders.

The best of hygiene to you,

Best Minister for Everything Nicely Perfect

The note dropped from Alice's fingers. She felt numb with shock. The Best Minister for Everything Nicely Perfect again! What was going on? Luckily, she'd snatched the Red Alert before Mrs Peasley could give it to Miss Grammaticus, so she was safe here for now, but for how long?

'Portland! Are you OK? We're waiting for you!'

Alice quickly shoved the envelope behind the wardrobe, undressed and climbed into the voluminous brown material. It was a bit, but not much, like a saggy swimsuit.

She pulled back the curtain.

'That's right,' said Chloe encouragingly, dressed in an identical suit. 'Come on, everyone's waiting.'

She took Alice to the toilets and led her into the end cubicle.

Alice stared.

Instead of the toilet there were two circular holes in the wall. One was labelled 'Grubby'. The other was labelled 'Clean'.

'Now slide!' instructed Chloe. 'Like this!' She stepped over the ledge of the Grubby hole, sat down and disappeared.

Alice rushed over.

The hole led to what looked like a water chute. Alice peered in disbelief. Yes, it was a water chute, leading off into a dazzling blue tunnel, with a stream of warm soapy water rushing down it.

'Hurry up!'

Behind her, the others had lined up, each wearing a similar baggy suit. Nervously, Alice sat down and pushed off. She slid faster and faster, looping round in a blue swirl. The soapy water made rainbow bubbles that clung to her.

Despite everything, despite the photo, despite the Pirus (whatever that was), Alice couldn't help laughing. This was so much better than being locked in her bedroom.

Then suddenly she shot out of the end and

dropped into swirling warm water.

'See – I told you it was a bathsuit!' shouted Chloe, her dark eyes shining.

Alice had never seen a bath like it. There were hundreds of children swimming and jumping in a big pool of green coloured waves. There was already a mass of foam on top of the water, but it rose higher and higher as more children dropped from the forest of chutes above.

'Professor Tryton built it. Luckily Miss Grammaticus reckons it's more time efficient for us all to have a bath together and kept it,' explained Chloe, floating in the foam. 'It washes your hair too.'

The foam was almost up to their heads by now. Alice lay back in the soapy suds, the bubbles gently tickling her. She couldn't stop giggling, but luckily no one could hear her over the splashing, fizzing and popping.

The bath was connected to the rinsing pool by a slope so wide that twenty children could slide together into the fresh carbolic-soap-scented water. Alice and Chloe spent a long time rinsing. They were still there when another bell clanged warningly.

'Spinning time! Come on!'

Chloe helped secure Alice into a wire alcove on a

large vertical wheel while Mrs Peasley waited impatiently. When the alcoves were full, the teacher cranked a giant handle and the wheel of cages spun very fast, flinging water everywhere. This made Alice sneeze quite badly, but luckily no one noticed.

'Blow dry now!' explained Chloe, and they stepped down into a dark tunnel, heads still spinning.

Warm air propelled Alice strongly forwards and upwards. By the time she'd half flown up their dormitory ladder and stepped out of the 'Clean' hole back into the toilet cubicle, she was giggling helplessly and perfectly dry.

'That's the bedtime bell,' said Chloe warningly, as a bell sounded. 'If we're not in bed by the second bell, we're in trouble. Mrs Peasley comes in after lights out to check on us.'

All around them, girls were scrambling into bed. Alice pulled on the mud-brown pyjamas that had mysteriously appeared on her bed during bathtime. Trying not to mind that she looked like she was wearing a baggy pillowcase, Alice climbed in under the covers and lay there, thinking.

The door opened. Alice pretended to be asleep. After a few moments she heard it close again.

'You OK?' whispered Chloe.

'Yeah,' Alice turned to face her. 'Chloe, how long have you been here?'

''Bout three years. I came when Professor Tryton was in charge. It was great then. We laughed all the time – even the lessons were fun. The Professor was fantastic. And staying in Tryton Mell was amazing . . . the best thing . . . well . . .' Chloe paused, struggling to explain, but Alice could see her face beaming in the dim light.

'But it's been terrible since Miss Grammaticus arrived,' Chloe added at last.

'You're not kidding,' whispered Emerald, who had been listening.

'I don't understand. Why didn't you all just leave as soon she came?'

'Coz it's impossible, Miss Grammaticus won't let us,' Chloe explained. 'Some of the others tried running away but they got caught.' She shuddered. 'Mrs Peasley loved punishing them for that.'

Alice puzzled over everything as she lay awake. What was the Pirus? What was it going to do to her? Why was the Best Minister so worried about it? What would happen to her here? How could she keep her nails squeaky clean?

It was a long time before she fell asleep.

CHAPTER SIX
In Miss Grammaticus's Study

'**W**ake up Maggott! The bell went five minutes ago!'

Alice awoke with a jerk. Someone had tugged her bedcovers off and was viciously shaking her shoulder. She had been having such a weird dream too, that a massive pie was chasing her, pushed by a giant woman shaking a duster and shouting...

She opened her eyes and groaned. The giant woman was looming above her. Alice shut her eyes quickly as a jug of cold water cascaded over her head.

'If you're not ready in five minutes and down with the others, Maggott . . .' Mrs Peasley didn't need to finish.

'Sorry,' Emerald said as the door closed. 'Here's your towel. We did try and wake you, but you were fast asleep. She comes in every morning, just after the bell . . . if you're not up . . . well, you know now . . .'

Alice nodded.

'You need to get a move on!' said Chloe, her face anxious. 'Come on!'

Alice got washed and dressed more quickly then she would ever have believed possible. Chloe expertly plaited Alice's hair and Emerald pulled her uniform straight so that it fell into the correct creases.

'Shame your hair's curly, and it's browny-ginger in places. I've gelled down the sticky out bits, but Miss Grammaticus might make you cut it all off if she spots the different colours, she hates imperfections,' said Chloe, her dark eyes anxious. Alice was beginning to realize that Chloe worried a lot.

'Don't worry, I've got some dark brown shoe

cream; I'll put it on and your hair will be perfect all over,' said Emerald, taking charge once again.

At the breakfast bell, Emerald led them out of the dormitory to a pair of polished wooden chutes on either side of the stairs – one marked 'BOYS' and one marked 'GIRLS'.

The sliding was great. By the time she had shot all the way down, racing the boys, Alice was giggling uncontrollably.

'Wipe that smirk off your face, Maggott, and move it!' ordered Trugg, poking Alice hard in the stomach. And as Alice bent double, wheezing with pain, Mrs Peasley appeared out of nowhere.

'Maggott! Miss Grammaticus wants you and Mudd to report to her study at eight o'clock sharp for assessment. Don't be late!'

Behind her, Alice could see blocks of frozen porridge being laid out for breakfast. Her heart sank, all giggles gone now. The day had started badly and it looked like it was going to get worse – much worse.

At 7.55 am exactly, Alice and Kevin tiptoed down an imposing blue-carpeted and pillar-lined hallway towards Miss Grammaticus's study.

'Look!' Kevin nudged Alice.

Alice saw it too, a human-sized cage firmly bolted to the wall next to the study door. The black metal bars looked unbreakable.

'You don't think she puts children in . . .' she said, horrified.

'Yeah I do . . . Better make sure we knock *exactly* on time,' Kevin replied, his eyes wide. And at that moment Alice heard footsteps.

'Shhh! It's her!'

They ducked behind a pillar as Miss Grammaticus glided to the keypad on her door.

'Let me see now . . . what's my door code? "Toad"?' she muttered. 'No, done T's, "Ugly"? No, that was last week, what are children this week? "Vile"! Yes, that's it!'

She keyed in the letters, turned the knob and walked into the study, the door lock clicking shut behind her.

Alice and Kevin exchanged agonized glances.

'It's ten seconds to eight o'clock, we'd better knock right now!' hissed Kevin.

Hand shaking, Alice tapped lightly on the door. Immediately, a loud intercom buzzed and the door clicked open.

'Here goes,' muttered Alice, turning the handle.

The study was cathedral-sized, so vast they could hardly see Miss Grammaticus's desk in the distance. But something else entirely made them goggle.

On every wall, from floor to ceiling, were shelves impossibly crammed with clocks. There were grandfather clocks, cuckoo clocks, tiny pocket watches and enormous station clocks, all perfectly synchronized and polished.

'There's gazillions!' Kevin whispered, awestruck.

And as they gaped, the clocks struck the hour together.

Bong! Bong! Bong! Bong! Bong! Bong! Bong! Bong!

'Oh – too loud!' gasped Alice, hastily covering her ears.

Apart from the clocks, the study was mostly a frosty white. Reluctantly they slid forward on the snowy carpet towards the desk.

Miss Grammaticus looked up, frowning.

'Ah, two miserable newbies. Well, at least you're on time. Punctuality and cleanliness, two qualities to be prized above all else. Come here!'

They obeyed at once.

Trying not to wake Precious, who was snoring by Miss Grammaticus's feet, they waited nervously in front of her desk while she finished writing. To distract herself, Alice studied the small faded photograph facing them.

What a rubbish picture, she thought, examining it. *I think it's supposed to be in colour, but you can't really tell, apart from the blue sky. Everything else in it's so black and white.*

She could make out four ghostly figures: a dark-haired girl and boy, and two grim-looking adults. They stood beside a house so bleak that it looked like a set from a horror movie.

Wow! That little girl must be Miss Grammaticus! Alice gasped, recognizing her icy expression immediately.

Just then, Precious twitched, opening one eye.

'Uh!' Kevin jumped, jarring the desk, and to their absolute horror the picture toppled face down on to the shiny wood.

In a panic, Kevin tried to set it back. Alice held her breath – perhaps he could sort it before Miss Grammaticus noticed.

But they were out of luck.

'Don't touch THAT!' Miss Grammaticus shrieked, leaping up and grabbing the photo from him. Brimming with anger, she snatched up a thick cane.

'OWWW!' Kevin howled as she smacked him furiously across his hand.

Miss Grammaticus lifted her cane again.

'What a lovely shiny desk, Miss Grammaticus – do you use pure beeswax polish?' Alice blurted out, desperate to distract the headmistress. She could see a nasty welt already blooming on Kevin's skin.

Miss Grammaticus paused, her arm still raised. Then to Alice's relief, she abruptly let the cane drop.

'So, two new children; both with filthy dirty names. I can tell you need to be here just from hearing them. Whose name is Mudd?'

'Mine,' said Kevin nervously.

Miss Grammaticus glared at him. 'I might have guessed. Children with terrible names are always trouble. How *dare* you touch my things with your grubby hands?'

She wiped the picture frame carefully, putting it down before turning to Alice.

'And you must be Maggott.'

Alice nodded unhappily.

'Well, which set shall I put you in? I've got to turn you into sparklingly perfect children, my reputation depends on that.' Miss Grammaticus glided round to stand directly over them. Alice felt an icy numbness creep up her legs.

'A-are there any tests?' asked Kevin bravely.

'Don't be silly, Mudd. I can tell just by looking at you.'

There was a moment of nervous silence, then . . .

'Mudd, you're a Dunce,' she said with satisfaction.

As Kevin crumpled in despair, the headmistress fixed Alice with her cold eyes. Alice's knees wobbled. Miss Grammaticus's stare was terrifying.

'Well, you do know your polishes, Maggott . . . your plaits are perfectly tied . . . and your hair's a flawless shade of brown . . . in fact, you're almost acceptable . . . Average, I think. I'll sign the forms.'

Alice and Kevin exchanged anguished glances. *We can't be separated, not now!* Alice thought. *We have to stick together.* She took a deep breath.

It was time to be brave.

'Miss Grammaticus, I think . . . you've made a mistake. I think Mudd's Average too.'

Miss Grammaticus and Kevin both goggled at her.

'Excuse me?' said the headmistress in a terrifyingly polite voice.

'I think . . .' Alice swallowed, her mouth dry. 'I think Mudd's Average too. Please may you test him again?'

Recovering, Miss Grammaticus smiled a slow evil smile.

'Well . . . if that's what you *really* want, Maggott.'

As they stared at her with increasing fear, she picked up two silver letter A badges and tossed both under her desk. To their horror, the letters struck Precious's nose.

He snarled viciously, hackles rising.

'If Mudd picks those badges up, I'll put you both in Average. If he fails, you're both Dunces. I think that's fair, don't you?'

Horrified, Alice opened her mouth to protest. Chloe had warned them about Precious. Kevin would be lucky to survive.

But Kevin got in first.

'Yeah, I'll do it,' he said, his face set.

'NO!' Alice pleaded.

Miss Grammaticus sniggered.

Desperate, Alice reached to grab Kevin, then hesitated, remembering how oddly Precious had behaved in the dining hall. She had been sure he was going to bite her, but he hadn't. Perhaps Kevin would be OK...

'Don't yer fret, Maggott; I can do this!' Kevin whispered white-faced, stepping shakily forward. The dog rose and lunged towards him, teeth bared.

'G-g-good d-d-dog,' Kevin stuttered.

Miss Grammaticus laughed.

'Be afraid,' she hissed. 'Be very afraid.'

Alice felt sick. Precious's snarls were deafening. *Please don't hurt him*, she pleaded silently. But just as she shut her eyes in despair, thinking Kevin was about to die, silence fell.

Alice opened one eye.

To her utter surprise, Precious was ignoring Kevin completely. Instead, he stood in front of her, his tail waving. And as she stared, he nudged her hand with his wet nose.

Tentatively, Alice patted him.

Precious collapsed on the floor with a sigh of pleasure, rolling over so that she could tickle his tummy.

Miss Grammaticus's eyes almost popped out of her head.

Alice didn't dare look at her. She stroked the

exposed belly and Precious's tail thumped on the ground, his eyes closing. Immediately, Kevin dived under the desk, grabbed the silver badges and scrambled hastily up, waving them triumphantly.

Miss Grammaticus sank down on to her chair, looking thunderous. Picking up a pen, she scrawled on two sheets of paper and stood up, clutching them tightly.

'Get out!' she hissed, grabbing Alice by her plaits and pulling her away from Precious and towards the door. 'Get out!'

She pushed Kevin out after Alice, thrusting the two forms into his hand before slamming the door shut.

As Kevin stood there, stunned, Alice extracted the forms and read them, a big grin spreading over her face.

Miss Grammaticus had ticked 'Average' on both.

CHAPTER SEVEN
A Little Bit of Rodent Trouble

Chloe was delighted. 'You'll both be sitting with me,' she said, as Alice happily pinned the silver letter 'A' to her blazer. 'We have to be in alphabetical order.'

Alice looked puzzled.

'Maggott, Merrikin and Mudd,' Chloe explained.

'Oh yeah, I keep forgetting I'm a Maggott,' Alice giggled, then immediately blushed. She needed to be careful – she'd nearly given herself away already.

Chloe gave her an odd look.

'What's now?' Alice hurriedly changed the subject.

'Miss Grammaticus's Mathematics is Perfectly Delightful lesson, she takes everyone at the same time,' Jago told her, sounding suspiciously cheerful.

Kevin groaned.

'Don't worry – it's only five times a week,' Chloe reassured him, as she showed them the way.

The classroom was massive, full of carved wood and marble walls. At the front were rows of brown uniformed children, sitting cross legged and silent. Alice could see they sat in age order, rising up from tiny children in front to miserable teenagers behind. All of them had a silver 'D' pinned on their blazers.

'They're the Dunces,' Chloe whispered.

Behind the Dunces were two long tables, lined with ruler-neat rows of worksheets. Only a few dozen pupils sat on the chairs here, and all wore silver 'A' badges.

'Hi!' Emerald said, looking impressed. 'You're with us then? How on earth did you wangle that?'

'Miss Grammaticus decided we looked Average,'

Alice said, sitting down. She caught Emerald's surprised stare and looked away hastily, badly wanting to giggle again.

'Coz Precious likes us,' Kevin added. Alice grinned at him.

Emerald glanced at them curiously. 'Tell us everything later,' she whispered.

'Shhh! She's coming!' warned Chloe.

Everyone fell silent instantly.

'Whole school mathematics – what a treat,' said Miss Grammaticus with a chilly smile as she strode in. 'Dunces! Tell me how nasty germs multiply when you use your dirty fingers to pick up your disgusting sweets.'

The Dunces began to chant dully.

'One, two, four, eight, sixteen, thirty-two, sixty-four, one hundred and twenty-eight . . .'

'What are they doing?' asked Alice.

'Chanting how the numbers of germs keep doubling on warm food as time passes,' whispered Emerald.

'Believe me, you'll know that off by heart soon,' said Oscar. 'You'll never look at a packed lunch in the same way again.'

'I'll be OK,' said Alice, thinking of how Mrs

Dent handled the bread for her sandwiches using tongs and wearing a mask and gown. 'My mum sterilizes all my sandwiches in the microwave, even—'

'Averages! Start your worksheets NOW!'

Alice hastily looked at hers, stuffing her fingers in her ears to block out the Dunces' chanting.

But it was no use. She couldn't concentrate, her ankle was itching badly. She reached down to scratch it and a small wet tongue licked her fingers.

A mouse!

'ARRRGH!' Alice screamed.

And as all eyes swivelled towards her, the mouse ran up her leg and under her tunic. Alice jumped up. Chloe, horrified, tried to grab her, but Alice pulled away, dashing for the door.

'MAGGOTT! SIT DOWN AT ONCE!' shrieked Miss Grammaticus.

Alice ignored her and raced on. She could feel tiny claws rock-climbing up her stomach.

But when Alice shakily extracted the white mouse in the toilets, he didn't scuttle off. Instead he smoothed his whiskers with tiny paws before scrambling up her leg again. Climbing on to her lap, he nuzzled her trembling fingers and rolled over to expose a pink tummy.

Alice stared at him. *He's quite sweet really,* she thought, watching his eager little nose twitching.

'You're supposed to be scared of people!' she told him, but the mouse ignored her, curling up contentedly on her tunic instead.

Mind you, after Precious and Cuddles, Alice was beginning to think there was something weird about the animals in Tryton Mell. They were all a bit odd and almost sticky, like glue.

The mouse really did seem attracted to her. Every time she tried to put him down, he came straight back, like she was a mouse magnet. *Wow – it's like having a pet dog,* thought Alice with growing excitement. Carefully, she stroked him with her hand. He nibbled her finger contentedly.

In the end, Alice settled him on a cosy bed of hand towels in her tunic pocket. She had read that mice often made terrible pets, but that didn't matter, because this mouse had definitely chosen her.

'I think I'll call you Nibbles,' she told him. And despite the fact that she was going to be in so much trouble if anyone found out, she couldn't help smiling.

Hastily washing her hands, she ran back to the hall.

'Miss Grammaticus, I'm sorry for disturbing

the class.'

Miss Grammaticus's eyes bulged. 'Top of the Naughty List tonight, Maggott – you can unblock the boys' toilets on the third floor!'

After Miss Grammaticus had left the room, the others crowded around Alice.

'Are you OK?' asked Chloe, her dark eyes worried.

'That was a brilliant yell,' Oscar looked at her in admiration.

'Yeah, sounded like yer chopped your leg off or something,' said Kevin, impressed.

'I'm fine,' said Alice hastily. She could feel her pocket moving; any minute now the mouse might pop up. Alice thought about showing him to the others, but that seemed risky. Right now she wasn't sure who she could trust.

'I just had stomach ache – I'm OK now. What's next?'

Jago pulled out his black notebook. 'I've got Advanced Engineering. You've got Pest Control.'

Alice groaned. The last thing she needed right now was a lesson in Pest Control. Not with a mouse hiding in her pocket.

On second thoughts though, given how weird

Tryton Mell animals were, maybe it was the very lesson she needed.

The Pest Control classroom was hidden in the deep dark depths of Tryton Mell.

'We just keep going down,' explained Chloe, as they whizzed downwards. By the time they tumbled off the last slide, Alice was giggling again. This seemed to upset Chloe quite a lot.

'You've got to stop that!' she whispered. 'Control it or you're going to get us all into so much trouble!'

'I can't help it!' protested Alice. *But at least my cold's going now,* she consoled herself. She'd finally stopped sneezing, which would have been great, if only her giggles weren't rapidly getting worse.

Chloe scowled.

'Portland – your peg's over here!' Emerald interrupted, holding out a dazzling white coat and plastic goggles. 'Put these on and make sure you shake your boots out first. I had a snake in mine once and Oscar squashed a frog last week.'

Alice looked doubtfully at the shiny white boots underneath her peg.

'Frogs aren't pests,' she objected.

'Obviously you've never had a plague of them,'

muttered Chloe.

'Everyone ready?' Oscar asked, before Alice could respond. And as they all nodded nervously, he pushed the round wooden door open.

The dark tunnel-like room beyond was filled from floor to ceiling with cages. Alice could see their teacher at the far end; a man – looking impeccably smart in a black velvet suit and shiny leather boots. His dark glittery eyes reminded her of a crocodile.

'That's Mr Anderson,' hissed Emerald.

'This is great!' whispered Kevin excitedly, eyeing the cages along the walls.

Alice looked around. The cages were all different sizes, big ones that had snouts and beaks poking through the bars, and smaller ones with inquisitive little heads popping out. Here and there were tanks filled with slimy things slithering around in deep green water.

'Don't squash the cockroaches!' Mr Anderson warned. 'I've let them out to hide so the Dunces can trap them in their lesson.'

Chloe screamed, jumping up as dark shadows scuttled across the floor towards them.

'Coward! Scared of a couple of insects!' Mr

Anderson sneered.

Chloe blushed. 'I hate insects and I hate this class,' she muttered.

Unfortunately Alice couldn't help giggling at this. Horrified, she muffled her mouth with her hand, but it was already too late. Chloe scowled at her and stalked off, which meant that Alice had to pair up with Kevin.

They ended up in the seats nobody else wanted, right at the front.

Uh-oh – not good, thought Alice, still desperately trying to stop more giggles escaping. She glanced uneasily at Mr Anderson, but he was too busy handing out small cages to notice.

Kevin poked their rattling cage curiously.

'Fizzing footballs! What in the—?'

'QUIET!'

Kevin jumped, shutting up at once as Mr Anderson surveyed the class. Everyone sat still, paying the teacher absolute attention.

'These animals are the nobility of the pest world, the kings of—'

'Oh my goodness – they're rats!' exclaimed Chloe faintly.

Alice stared at the two brown heads that had just

popped out of the cage in front of them. They stared back with coal black eyes, their little noses twitching.

'Yes, they're rats – but rats are capable of wiping out entire populations, so this lesson is a very dangerous place to be.' As they stared at him in horror, Mr Anderson lovingly caressed the nearest cage. 'We've had these rats in quarantine and sterilized their bedding, but they could still carry mortal diseases. However, if you wear your gloves and wash your hands properly afterwards, you might just live. Now, everyone take out a rat and examine them carefully.'

'No way!' whispered Chloe. But everyone else apart from Alice and Kevin dived straight in.

There was instant pandemonium.

The rats wriggled and jumped and bit fingers hard. Soon escaped rats were darting everywhere.

'Well . . . s'pose we'd better get on with it,' said Kevin brightly, lifting up the cage top. But as soon as the door was open, both animals jumped at Alice.

'ARRRGH! – get them OFF!' she shrieked, grabbing Kevin in panic. She couldn't believe it; including the mouse in her pocket, she now had *three* rodents stuck to her!

'Don't fuss, they're brilliant!' said a sharp-faced boy walking past, his rat perched happily on his shoulder.

'Yeah, trust you to like rats, Henry *Rat*-tenbury!' called Oscar from the next table.

'GET THEM OFF ME!'

This was difficult. The rats clung to Alice with tiny paws and didn't take kindly to being dislodged. What made matters ten times worse was that Henry Rattenbury's rat preferred Alice too.

'Well that helped,' said Alice crossly, as all three rats lined up on her shoulder, curling their tails around her plaits for balance.

'Sorry but I think they must really like you – p'raps you've got a ratty smell.' Henry plucked back his own rodent and walked away, grinning.

Alice stared after him. She actually didn't mind the rats, now she'd got over the shock. But why had they jumped on her like that? *It's not just the rats!* she thought uneasily. In fact she was going to have to add rats to the growing list of animals attracted to her. Alice ticked them off in her mind: Cuddles, Precious, Nibbles and now three rats.

There really is something weird about the animals here, she mused as Kevin finally manged to peel both rats off her and stuff them back into their cage.

But then again, no one else seemed to be having similar trouble.

She couldn't ignore the truth any longer: it was glaring right at her. *It's not the animals: it's me!* she thought. A chill of terror trickled down her spine.

'You both OK?' asked Chloe as they left the classroom. Now that Pest Control was over, she was back to her usual friendly self. 'You don't want to ignore bites, he's right, rats can carry terrible diseases.'

'Yeah, we're fine, coz rats just love her,' Kevin pointed to Alice. 'But it's mega-odd how they jumped on yer like that. Do yer keep rats?'

Alice shook her head quickly. 'Maybe they liked the smell of shoe cream on my hair,' she retorted, and hurried off up the stairs to get ready for punishment chores before the others could respond.

Things were getting more and more out of hand. Alice felt that until she'd worked out what was going on and who to trust, the less the others knew about her sticky animal problem the better.

CHAPTER EIGHT
Solutions and Problems

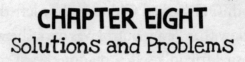

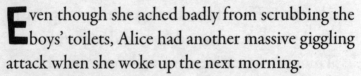

Even though she ached badly from scrubbing the boys' toilets, Alice had another massive giggling attack when she woke up the next morning.

'Stop that!' Emerald ordered, pulling the bedclothes off and shaking her shoulders roughly. Alice giggled harder. She just couldn't help it.

'Please stop! You'll be in so much trouble if Mrs Peasley catches you!' pleaded Chloe.

'Let's shove something in her mouth, that'll shut

her up,' said Emerald in desperation. Alice gulped and jumped out, closing her mouth quickly before anyone got any ideas.

Just in time.

Mrs Peasley had arrived.

'Well well, so you're out of bed with the bell this morning, you measly little Maggott. Being on the Naughty List obviously suits you.'

Alice kept her mouth shut. She could feel more giggles rising up.

'You're going purple,' said Mrs Peasley with interest. 'A jug of ice-cold water over your head will soon sort that.'

But even with her hair soaking wet, Alice had more fits of giggles all the way through dressing. Chloe had to help her with her plaits again.

'For goodness' sake! Pull yourself together, Portland!' said Emerald crossly, as she made them all line up.

With a massive effort, Alice managed to stop until she had slid down the chutes. It was really odd – even though the Best Minister was after her, Mrs Peasley and Miss Grammaticus were so horrible, and she had a rogue mouse in her pocket – there were moments when she felt so happy she thought she might burst.

'Don't you dare start giggling again!' Emerald warned Alice as they sat down to breakfast.

'We've all got Solutions this morning,' said Chloe happily, chipping away at her frozen orange juice with a knife.

'Good, coz I got a lot of problems right now,' said Kevin, who was looking miserable. He had tried to ring his mum from the phone box in the entrance hall, but Mrs Peasley had caught him.

'Just had time to say "hi Mum" before she hauled me out,' he said bitterly. 'Did yer know she listens in to all calls?'

He slid into his seat, burying himself in a crumpled letter he pulled from his pocket. Noticing it was signed '*with love and hugs, Mum xxxxxx*', Alice's giggles vanished at once. She felt sorry for Kevin, but she couldn't help feeling a pang of envy. Kevin's mum sounded lovely, not at all like hers. Alice had never been hugged – Mrs Dent firmly believed that touching germ-ridden children was dangerous.

Chloe leant over and patted Kevin's shoulder apologetically.

'Sorry, we should have warned you about Mrs

Peasley. And it's not that kind of solutions – more like mixtures,' she added.

Kevin looked up, puzzled.

'Don't ask me,' Alice told him. 'I have no idea what she's on about.'

The Solutions room turned out to be a kitchen in the oldest part of Tryton Mell. The large, low-ceilinged room was brightly cheerful, despite having tiny diamond windows and wonky walls. Gleaming black stoves stood in rows on the polished red flagstone floor.

'Let's bag this one,' said Chloe, standing by a stove right at the front.

'This is the only lesson where you can get away with making a mess,' Oscar confided to Alice. He was at the hob behind them with Jago and Emerald.

'Wear these.' Chloe handed Alice a luminous green apron and hairnet. Alice looked at the colour doubtfully, but everyone else was glowing too.

'Nice outfit,' said Kevin, grinning, as Alice tucked her plaits in.

Before Alice could retort, there was a loud bang and a man strode in, carrying an enormous black pot.

'Who's that?' Alice asked Chloe.

'Mr Pye,' Chloe whispered. 'He's the only teacher left from when Professor Tryton was here.'

Alice's stomach flipped over.

'What's wrong? You've gone white!'

'Nothing,' said Alice, but that was untrue. Mr Pye's name had reminded her about the Pirus. How could she have forgotten? *I'm safe here for now, no one knows who I really am,* Alice reassured herself. But she knew that wouldn't last.

It was difficult to see Mr Pye behind the steam billowing from the bubbling liquid, but he was tall, with thick-rimmed glasses and the sort of face that gave nothing away. Alice could see why Miss Grammaticus liked him, his perfect hair and shoes gleamed from polishing and his white overalls were dazzling. Many of the teachers wore these overalls, but Mr Pye's were special, like fluffy clouds in a blue sky.

'Right, settle down, everyone,' Mr Pye instructed, putting the round-bellied pot on the stove. 'Goggles on and line up in front of me, quickly now!'

Chloe pulled Alice and Kevin forward.

'Ah, Merrikin,' said the teacher, towering above them. 'And who's this?'

'Portland Maggott and Kevin Mudd, sir – they've just arrived.'

'But good enough to be Averages already,' said Mr Pye, staring at them with curious eyes.

'Portland's very clever,' replied Kevin cheerfully, pointing at Alice. She glared at him, but the teacher just smiled.

'Well, we'll soon see about that. Right everyone, put out the hand you don't write with.' He picked up a thermometer and slid it into the pot, checking the reading.

'OK, dip your hand in the cauldron all of you Averages; it's cool enough now.'

Chloe stepped forward and thrust her hand into the tarry liquid. When she pulled her hand out it was coated in thick black goo.

'You too, Maggott – hurry up!'

Alice reached in. The gloopy mixture was warm and smelt of liquorice. It felt nice against her fingers; she was never allowed to get her hands dirty normally.

'That's permanent stain mixture,' explained Mr Pye. 'Nothing will get it off except a super-duper stain remover. You need to make one in this morning's lesson if you want clean hands before you leave.'

'But it's hand inspection before lunch!' said Chloe, her eyes wide. 'We'll be in so much trouble!'

Mr Pye laughed. 'I know – fun isn't it! Nothing makes a lesson pass more quickly than a bit of real life danger, don't you think? Now, as usual, I'm trusting you to get on quietly without me. There are recipes for different stain removers on these worksheets. One of them will work, but you haven't got time to try them all so choose well. You can use any ingredient . . .' he waved his arms towards the cupboards around the walls.

'Come on,' said Chloe, grabbing a handful of worksheets and towing Alice back to their stove. 'We've got a lot to do and not much time.'

Alice looked at the sheet curiously. There were five different lists of ingredients, all with instructions like in a cookbook.

'Want to work together?' asked Oscar. 'We could do one each.'

'Yes, if we double the quantities then there should be enough for all five of us,' said Chloe.

'There's six of . . .' Alice tailed off, noticing that Jago's hands were still impeccibly clean.

'Don't worry about me,' he reassured her. 'I'm

doing Gleaming Genius work. I have to invent a potion that kills nits but is harmless to pupils when they drink it. Mrs Peasley's planning to try it out tomorrow.'

'But . . . you could kill us all!'

'Precisely, so don't interrupt me – I need to concentrate.'

Nevertheless, Jago couldn't resist checking over Alice and Kevin's work and telling them exactly what to do. Secretly, Alice was glad about this; making a good concoction was a lot harder than it seemed.

At last, two hours later, everyone was finished.

'OK, they're cool enough, let's try them,' said Emerald, dubiously eyeing the steaming liquids.

They heaved their pots on to the middle work bench. Chloe's and Kevin's mixtures were thick and brown, one toffee-scented, the other smelling of trainers. Emerald's was watery green and Oscar's fizzed slightly.

'On the count of three then,' instructed Jago, peering into their pots with interest 'One . . . two . . . THREE!'

Each of them plunged their hands into their

own pot. Alice gave her yellow sludge a good stir, but wasn't surprised to see that the black crust was still there when she pulled her hand out. Chloe, Emerald, and Kevin were looking disappointed too, but Oscar stared unbelievingly at his sparkling pink hand.

'Way to go, Os!' cheered Kevin as they all crowded around his pot.

'Well well,' said Mr Pye, reappearing just as the bell clanged. 'Looks like you Averages might survive hand inspection after all.'

At lunch, Alice was so busy thinking that she didn't even notice she was eating frozen turnips. How long would it be before someone noticed her animal problem or that she couldn't stop giggling? Thank goodness her cold had finally cleared up, but how long did she have before anyone realized that Portland Maggott didn't exist?

She could feel Nibbles rooting around in her pocket. How on earth could she keep him hidden? And there was the Pirus. How did that fit in?

Up to now Alice had tried not to think about the Pirus or the Best Minister, but she had a horrible feeling that she was in terrible and growing danger.

And what if the Best Minister sent another Red Alert? This time she wouldn't be there to stop it getting to Miss Grammaticus. She was really scared now; things were getting rapidly worse and she didn't know what to do.

'You OK, Portland?' asked Chloe.

Alice made up her mind. She couldn't deal with this on her own. She needed help, fast. As everyone else got up to clear tables, she pulled Kevin, Chloe and Jago aside.

'Listen,' she said. 'I've got something tell you. My name's not really Portland Maggott.'

CHAPTER NINE
The Dusty Side

Kevin, Chloe and Jago gawped at Alice.

'What do yer mean yer not Portland Maggott?' asked Kevin, looking bewildered.

'Shhh!' Alice hissed. 'Can we talk somewhere private?'

Jago turned to Chloe. 'What do you think?' he asked her.

'Let's take them to the Dusty Side,' said Chloe mysteriously.

'You think we can trust them with that?'

'Of course yer can!' said Kevin indignantly as Chloe nodded.

'OK, we just need to distract Mr Ricard— hey!'

Jago ducked – Kevin had flipped a frozen sprout into the middle of the Dunces, triggering a hail of leftover potatoes back in retaliation.

'That'll keep him busy,' exclaimed Kevin, watching Mr Ricard and the Perfect Poppets sprint down the hall toward the shrieking Dunces.

'Good enough,' acknowledged Jago, as they slipped out unnoticed.

When they reached the deserted entrance hall, Jago stopped in front of the giant fireplace and peeled back one corner of the plastic sheeting that sealed the opening.

He pointed up the chimney.

'It's up there.'

Alice and Kevin looked at each other.

'Yer joking, right?'

'No he's not – look, I'll show you.' Chloe stepped into the fireplace, lifted her arms and disappeared upwards.

'Your turn,' said Jago. 'I'll go last.'

'OK.' Kevin ducked inside the chimney and started climbing, Alice following him nervously. Inside the fireplace were lots of overlapping broad shelves leading upwards, like a ladder for giant snakes.

'It's just like soft-play,' Kevin said happily. 'Used ter take the babies all the time with me mum.'

'See – told you it was easy,' said Chloe, as they reached the top. She shook dust out of her red-brown plaits.

'Where *are* we?' asked Alice, climbing out of the chimney through a door in a smaller fireplace. The door was labelled with the words '**Fire Exit**'.

Chloe grinned. 'Welcome to the Dusty Side!'

Alice looked around. The huge room was lined with a jumble of books on shelves that stretched from the ceiling to the floor. A wooden balcony ran around the room, reached by a stout ladder. But in among the shelves were dozens of doors, some narrow and tall, others square and small. A few were round or odd shaped. Every door was labelled.

She read the nearest.

Kitchen . . . Maze . . . The Windy Gap . . . Tree-house . . . Secret Tower. . . Foxhole . . . Spiral Corridor . . . The Bog . . . Way for the Warrior . . .

'Hey, some of these labels are like them signs on the blocked-off corridors!' Kevin exclaimed excitedly.

'What *is* this place?' asked Alice.

'The old library,' explained Jago. 'You can get to anywhere from here. Miss Grammaticus doesn't know anything about it. There's no regular door in, so she's never found it.'

'Most of the others don't know about it either,' Chloe added. She and Jago lounged on two big blue sofas, watching Alice and Kevin explore. 'Professor Tryton built two libraries; a big one downstairs and this one as a secret that only children who really wanted adventure or to escape would find. It's a good thing he did; Miss Grammaticus burnt all the books in the other library. She said they were germ carriers, spreading bugs from pupil to pupil.'

'Is that why we don't have textbooks?' asked Alice, who had thought this odd.

'Precisely,' said Jago.

'I bet it were a laugh here before Miss Grammaticus,' said Kevin, still browsing the mysterious doors set between the shelves.

'It was brilliant,' Chloe told him, smiling at the memory.

'When did she come?'

'About nine months ago. Professor Tryton was in charge before then, he was great.'

'Where's he gone?'

'He disappeared the same night Miss Grammaticus arrived. He refused to let her in, but then all these men came in long black cars and battered the door down. They tried to grab him, but he fought them off and escaped through the maze. We saw the whole thing through the dormitory windows – Miss Grammaticus was furious,' Chloe smiled at the memory. 'When we came down the next morning she'd already made herself headmistress. She put us in this uniform and started perfect pupil classes straight away.'

'Don't you have inspections and stuff? Are they happy with all this?' asked Alice.

'They love it,' said Chloe gloomily. 'And the staff don't care. Miss Grammaticus got rid of Professor Tryton's teachers and hired her own.'

'Except Mr Pye,' said Jago.

'Yeah, like he's going to stand up to Miss Grammaticus,' Kevin snorted.

'They're all so horrible,' said Alice. 'They're like big bullies.'

'They're not happy,' said Chloe. 'Bullies are never happy. Have you ever seen Miss Grammaticus smile?'

'Look!' exclaimed Kevin, opening the Foxhole door. A steel ladder disappeared downwards into blackness. He tried the next, labelled Sick Bay. This had a steep-sided slide covered in thick cobwebs.

'One way trip only I guess,' said Alice, as they peered in.

Unlike the rest of Tryton Mell, there was dust on the bookshelves. The room had a warm, cosy feel, with its faded red and black carpet and big wooden tables.

'We're safe here,' said Chloe. 'Now sit down and tell us everything.'

Alice threw herself on to a sofa and looked at the others. Chloe was flushed pink, her plaits undone, but Jago was still neat, his black hair firmly in place. There wasn't a speck of dirt on him. Kevin looked like he'd been swimming in dust.

She took a deep breath. Jago and Chloe had trusted her with their secret. She had to trust them with hers.

'Well, I got this nasty cold . . .' she began.

Alice told them everything that had happened, beginning with being locked in her bedroom.

She told them about having to escape, the police capturing her and the papers she'd taken from Mrs Peasley's office. She took out the Best Minister's letter and Red Alert from their hiding place in her blazer lining.

The others listened in stunned silence, passing the paper sheets to each other like they were bombs about to explode.

And as they gazed at her in shock, Nibbles chose that moment to shift in his nest.

'Your . . . your blazer's moving,' said Chloe faintly.

'Yeah . . . that's another thing.' Alice dug Nibbles out of her pocket and put him on the table.

'What the . . ?' Chloe moved hastily backwards.

The mouse stared at them, sitting on his hind legs and washing his face. He then strolled back to Alice and rolled over, pawing at her to tickle his tummy.

Chloe was the first to break the silence. 'What on earth's going on? First Precious, now this. And Henry said he couldn't get the rats off you in Pest Control. Are you some sort of animal magnet?'

Alice looked at her with frightened eyes. 'I don't know what's happening. I love animals, but this . . .

this thing's never happened to me before – they seem to stick to me like glue now. I can't get rid of Nibbles, he keeps coming back.' Alice stroked his back gently. 'I do like him, but I'll be in serious trouble if anyone spots him.'

'Fizzing footballs! What's going on?' exclaimed Kevin, bewildered.

Jago was still scrutinizing the Best Minister's letter.

'I think this Pirus might be the key to everything. I wonder what it does?'

'Are yer going to die?' Kevin asked, inspecting Alice with interest.

'Shut up, Kevin,' Chloe ordered.

'If I do,' countered Alice, 'you'll be next. If it's infectious, you lot might already have it.'

'Wouldn't we be ill now though?' asked Chloe. 'I feel fine but you had a runny nose and cough when you first came. I'm surprised Mrs Peasley didn't notice you sneezing. Wouldn't I have a cold by now if that was the Pirus?'

'Not yet maybe.' Jago looked Alice up and down. Alice was beginning to feel like she was in the zoo. 'It depends how long the incubation period is.'

'Hold it – what the heck is that?' asked Kevin.

'The time it takes from picking up a germ to the

time it makes you ill. It's a few days for a common cold, but two to three weeks for chickenpox and it can be months for some infections.'

'Yer mean we might already be brewing this Pirus but not show it?' Kevin looked horrified.

'And we don't have any idea how long this . . . this . . . incubation is?' Chloe added.

'Exactly,' said Jago.

'It might be a mistake,' said Alice hopefully. 'I feel fine now – maybe I just had a cold that went on for ages. You can get false results on tests sometimes, can't you?'

There was silence for quite a while as the others thought hard. Then Jago and Chloe exchanged looks.

'Is she really telling us the truth?' Jago asked, ignoring Alice.

Chloe nodded. 'I'm sure she is.'

'Well thanks very much!' said Alice indignantly. 'Anyway, forget being infectious – it's the Best Minster for Everything Nicely Perfect that's really freaking me out. What does he want with me? I wish I knew more about him.'

'He's always on telly, wearing black,' said Kevin, 'standing next to the Prime Minister . . .'

'That's no help, I don't have a TV or radio. Mum thinks static electricity attracts germs,' Alice told him.

'The newspapers say the Best Minister insists something terrible will happen if people don't follow his new rules,' Jago explained. 'I wonder if it might be this Pirus – I've not heard of it before. It would explain why he's so obsessed with germs and making sure that everyone's clean.'

'But why's he clamping down on laughing and giggling as well?' asked Alice. 'What's that got to do with this Pirus? What's wrong with being happy?'

Jago shrugged his shoulders. 'I don't know. All I know is that he puts his mark on everything that follows his new rules. Tryton Mell's officially approved by him; that's why we wear his badge.' Jago pointed to the shield on Alice's blazer.

'I guessed that,' Alice said, an icy trickle sliding down her spine. For days she'd been trying not to think about it, but now Jago had reminded her again.

'Yeah, so what's it matter if he's involved?' Kevin asked Jago.

'The Best Minister's very dangerous,' continued

Jago quietly. 'You're in deep trouble if he's after you. Last winter he got cross with some school children dropping litter in Trafalgar Square. They're still lost in the Sahara desert.'

'I don't want to end up in a desert – I get bad sunburn if I even see the sun!' Alice protested.

'I think it'll be something far worse,' said Jago. 'This letter suggests he's really out to get you. My uncle met the Best Minister once. When he came back he was shaking all over and I heard him tell my dad that the Best Minister's the most evil man he's ever met.'

'Jago – that's not helpful.' Chloe frowned at him.

'I've got to find out exactly what's going on.' Alice was really upset now. 'If the Pirus doesn't kill me first it sounds like the Best Minister will find me and kill me instead. I can't hide for much longer.'

She stopped, choking back tears. Nibbles licked her finger, just like a dog. Strangely comforted by this, Alice cradled him gently in her hand.

Chloe was reading the letter again. 'It says here there's an antidote to the Pirus. Perhaps if you took that . . .'

Alice stared at her. 'The Pirus antidote – I'd

forgotten about that! That would solve everything! But how can I find it, I wouldn't know where to start . . . even the Best Minister's struggling . . .'

'Let's make a list of what you need to do,' said Jago. 'That always helps.'

He pulled out his notebook. Alice watched as he wrote in perfect handwriting:

1. Find out about the Pirus
2. Hide from the Best Minister for Everything Nicely Perfect
3. Find the antidote

'Anything else?' Jago clipped the top back on his pen. They were all concentrating so hard on Jago's list that it was surprising that it didn't burst into flames.

'It's difficult when we don't know anything about this Pirus,' Chloe pointed out.

'Can't we look it up in them books?' asked Kevin. 'Or on a computer?'

'Miss Grammaticus smashed all the computers,' Chloe told him. 'She reckons touch screens and keyboards are germ factories. The only computer left is in Mrs Peasley's office.'

Alice shook her head. 'It'll be useless to do a

search on Pirus; the Best Minister's bound to have blocked anything about it.'

'Yeah, or he'll trace it as coming from here and start investigating,' added Chloe, her eyes wide.

'I agree. Then there's only one way forward,' said Jago. 'We need to find a Public Health doctor.'

The others stared at him in bewilderment.

'What's one of them?' asked Kevin.

'Public Health stops horrible infections spreading between people. They came to our school last year because all the prefects suddenly got terrible rashes. I asked the doctors and nurses loads of questions and they told me how Public Health investigates odd things, so they're bound to know about the Pirus,' Jago explained. 'I suggest we break out, track down the nearest Public Health doctor and make them tell us what's going on.'

'Frazzling fruitcakes! That'll be easy,' Kevin murmured, but Jago totally missed the sarcasm.

'Yes, it will be, won't it – we just need a plan,' Jago told him, his eyes lighting up. 'Now . . . if you three distract Mrs Peasley at bath time, I'll sneak into her office, find her computer, crack her password, identify the nearest Public Health doctor and find where they live. Then tonight we'll go to bed as normal and sneak out when everyone's asleep. All we need to do after that is get to the right house, force the doctor to answer our questions and get back here before anyone notices we're missing. It's so simple, what could go wrong?'

For a moment they were too stunned to speak.

Kevin recovered first. 'Yeah, really nice and simple. We should fit that in before bedtime.' He shook his head in amazement. 'Wow, yer really off the wall, mate.'

But to Alice and Kevin's surprise, Chloe agreed with Jago.

'It's the only logical thing to do. We can plan everything properly in Dicing with Death Cookery this afternoon – Mr Pye teaches that too and he usually leaves us alone.'

'It's my problem,' Alice protested, not liking the sound of Jago's plan at all. 'You shouldn't get involved. We could all end up in serious trouble.'

'It's too late, we're already involved. No, Public Health's our best option for now.'

And Alice had no answer to that.

'What'll we wear?' Chloe asked hesitantly. 'We've only got school uniform. If we turn up wearing that they'll know we've escaped.'

'Pyjamas of course,' replied Jago, as though this was obvious. Kevin rolled his eyes.

Despite her worries, Alice giggled. 'Forget being forced to talk, it's the pyjamas that'll really freak the public health doctor out!'

CHAPTER TEN
A Little Friendly Night Visiting

'Nice pyjamas!' grinned Kevin when they met up at midnight. They were all wearing identical shapeless outfits, and Alice had to admit that Jago was right. Their baggy brown school pyjamas were more like badly made tracksuits than nightclothes.

Much to their amazement, Jago's plan had worked perfectly.

'How on earth did you work out Mrs Peasley's password?' Alice asked him in awe.

Jago shrugged. 'Easy, for a Genius like me,' he replied. 'It was obviously Miss-Grammaticus-Is-Perfect.'

This made Alice want to giggle quite badly, but the others soon shut her up.

'I'm scared!' whispered Chloe, as they crept nervously through the dark corridors.

'Yer fine, no one's gonna be up,' Kevin told her, but he was wrong. At the entrance hall, Jago abruptly halted them.

'Look!' he hissed, pointing.

Alice's heart almost exploded – Mrs Peasley's office door was slightly ajar, with yellow light spilling outwards.

'Oh no! She's still awake! What's she doing?'

'Probably thinking of new ways to torture us,' Kevin whispered.

They crept forward very gingerly. As they drew level with the open door, Alice felt sick. She could see Mrs Peasley inside, humming happily as she polished her dusting trophies.

Chloe gulped in terror.

Mrs Peasley paused, lifting her head suspiciously. Terrified, they all dived back into the shadows, just as Mrs Peasley strode to her door and peered out.

Hurriedly, Kevin pulled something from his pocket and tossed it upwards. It landed with a click in the corridor opposite and Mrs Peasley immediately scuttled off to investigate.

And as soon as she disappeared out of the hall, they dashed for the front door.

'What was that?' hissed Jago.

'Rat treat from Pest Control – knew it would come in handy.'

Alice felt giggles rising up.

'Don't start!' warned Chloe as she slid back the huge door bolts. 'I'll wait here and cover up for you if there's trouble,' she promised, just as they had planned earlier.

'I calculate we'll be back in exactly four hours,' instructed Jago. 'Be here then – we need you to let us back in.'

Chloe nodded.

'Good luck,' she whispered, closing the door behind them.

'How do we get over *that*?' asked Alice, when they reached the boundary wall.

'Use these to catch that tree branch and swing

over,' said Jago, plucking something out of a nearby bush.

Alice stared.

'No way!' she protested.

Jago was holding several pairs of trainers with enormous springs attached to their soles.

'I made them in my Advanced Engineering class,' he said proudly.

'Yer off your rocker if yer think we're wearing them,' said Kevin.

'Theoretically, they work!' Jago protested, sounding hurt. 'I've done all the calculations!'

Kevin swore loudly. 'All right, show us. If we're not picking bits of yer splattered over the wall, we'll 'ave a go.'

Jago laced up the trainers, stood up and began to run.

'Wow, that's amazing!' said Alice, as Jago rose higher with each bound. He sprung up into the air, caught the tree branch easily and swung over the wall.

Kevin swore again. 'That's a blinking miracle!'

Alice had three goes before she managed to scramble over. As she lay gasping on the grass, Kevin landed lightly at her feet.

He hauled Alice upright.

'Ups-a-daisy Sunshine!'

Alice refused to speak to either of them all the way down the lane. Instead she stroked Nibbles, who was still quivering from being bounced.

'Where are we going exactly?' Kevin asked Jago. 'I don't do walking – take me bike mostly.'

'Snowdrop Cottage, in Slugsend. It's only five miles away, we'll be there in one hour and fifteen minutes if we walk at the recommended postal service speed,' said Jago.

'Five miles!' Kevin looked about to faint.

This made Alice giggle a lot.

Snowdrop Cottage was the sort of cottage you saw on holiday postcards, all pretty yellow walls under a thatched roof.

'Go on – I'll keep watch and rescue yer if there's trouble.' Kevin crouched behind the hedge as Jago knocked.

It was ages before the door was opened. At last a stern-looking lady, clad in an orange flowery dressing gown, cautiously peered out.

'Oh, just children!' she said, sounding relieved. 'What do you want?'

'We need to talk to Dr Goodish-Leech,' said Jago in a solemn grown-up voice.

'I'm Dr Goodish-Leech,' the woman told him.

Jago looked puzzled. 'You don't look like the photo of Dr Goodish-Leech on the computer,' he objected.

'Perhaps you saw my husband's picture,' the woman smiled. 'We're both Public Health doctors so people often muddle us up. What do you want?'

'We want the truth about the Pirus,' said Jago. Alice tried to kick him to shut him up but it was too late.

The woman looked wary. 'You'd better come in,' she said, holding the door open. 'Digby!' she called up the stairs. 'There are some young people here who want to talk to us!'

'What, Diana . . .? Who?' Dr Digby Goodish-Leech stumbled sleepily down the stairs wearing orange-striped pyjamas.

'We don't mean any harm,' said Alice quickly as they moved into the sitting room. 'I just need to know what's going on.'

Dr Digby picked up a pair of glasses, rammed them on and peered at her closely.

'Alice Dent!' he exclaimed, recoiling.

'Y-y-yes,' said Alice, too surprised to deny it.

'Alice Dent?' asked his wife, her eyes widening. 'No way!'

Leaping backwards, she stared hard at Alice. 'Yes . . . I can see it is now. But that brown hair colour makes you look so different, especially with such neat plaits and your shiny scrubbed face.'

'How did you know it was me?' Alice asked Dr Digby.

'All of us Public Health experts in nasty infections have been studying your photograph for days. I recognized your eyes – those bright amber flecks against that vivid blue are quite unusual,' said Dr Digby, busily flinging open all the windows. He hurried over to a large cupboard, wrenched the door open, pulled out a box and grabbed a fistful of blue surgical masks. Strapping one over his face with trembling fingers and handing another to Dr Diana, he threw two towards Alice and Jago.

'Put these on and stand over there!'

Alice tied the mask over her mouth and nose.

'What's wrong with me?' she asked.

'You're infected,' said Dr Digby, as though that explained everything.

'Yes, well I guessed that,' said Alice impatiently.

'But what with?'

'Ah, that's the problem. You're shedding a Positive Virus ... a Pirus.'

'A Positive Virus!' exclaimed Alice. 'Is that bad?'

'It's very bad!'

'But I feel fine!' she protested.

'You just wait – probably too early yet for the worst symptoms.'

'Will I die?' Alice was really frightened now.

'Oh, I'd say that's highly unlikely. These Positive Viruses are a bit like common cold viruses.' He stopped, considering. 'Actually, nothing like common cold viruses. Except that they're both very infectious.'

'What does a Pirus do to you?' asked Jago curiously.

'When you catch one, it changes you for the better. Let me see now, some examples ... there's the Carrot Pirus, good for eyesight, and the Jester Pirus, good for making up incredibly fantastic jokes. And there's the Flower Pirus, which makes people peace- ful. Last time that came round it infected millions of youngsters; they did nothing but lie around all day singing. And let's not forget the Wow Pirus, good for—'

'Yes, thank you, Digby, they get the picture,' interrupted Dr Diana Goodish-Leech, frowning at him. Alice got the impression that the doctors weren't supposed to talk about Piruses.

'But what's so bad about them? They sound great!' she exclaimed.

'Well—' said Dr Digby, but his wife cut him off abruptly.

'Never mind about that. Have you noticed anything odd yet?'

'Odd?' asked Alice nervously. 'What sort of odd?' She could feel Nibbles stirring in her pocket. *Having a mouse in my pocket, well, that's quite odd, and then there's Cuddles and Precious . . .* She pushed the thoughts hastily away.

'Well, is anything strange happening to you?'

Jago looked at Alice's pocket, then opened his mouth. Alice stood on his foot, hard. She didn't think it would be a good idea for Jago to reveal everything right now.

'Nothing *really* strange,' she said quickly, ignoring Jago's surprised face. 'Which Pirus have I got?'

'Yours is related to the Snortle virus, I've been told,' said Dr Digby. 'One of the most dangerous.'

'The *what*?' interrupted Jago.

'The Snortle virus, named after Professor R. B. Snortle, who discovered it. It makes you happy.'

'Happy! So why's it so dangerous?'

'It's unpredictable and has very odd effects. It starts with a horrible cold, like many viruses, and then has different effects in children and adults. Almost immediately, grown-ups become very happy all the time. Some just sit around smiling all day, others do strange things; usually what they've always secretly wanted to do but never dared. In the last Pirus epidemic, for example, there were reports of an old lady building a tree house and throwing ice-cream snowballs at passers-by.'

'What about children?' interrupted Alice, not sure she really wanted to know.

'Giggling attacks.'

'Giggling attacks?'

'Yes, annoying fits of giggles.' Dr Digby Goodish-Leech spoke slowly. 'Odd little bouts of being incredibly happy, which makes them laugh and giggle, and then . . . I'm surprised you haven't had any yet.'

But I have! Alice thought, going cold all over. She couldn't deny it any longer. It wasn't a mistake. There was no doubt about it now; she definitely had this Pirus.

She could see Jago staring at her, horrified. She guessed he was also remembering all the giggling attacks she had had lately.

'Go on!' Jago demanded. He and Alice were on the edge of their seats.

'Then after a week or two weird things start happening. Piruses seem to have a deeper effect on children.'

'Weird things? Like what?'

Dr Digby shrugged his shoulders. 'Nobody knows what after-effects your Pirus has but I'm sure you'll find out soon enough . . . Hopefully nothing too bad but there are some alarming reports from the last epidemic . . . '

The Pirus must be what's made me an animal magnet! Alice realized with a shock. That wasn't so bad, she really liked having animals attracted to her, but how much worse would it get? Everyone was bound to notice if packs of animals started following her everywhere. But what if it attracted things like snakes and tarantulas? And the giggling was getting worse too; surely it was dangerous to laugh so much? Sometimes she couldn't even catch her breath for giggling.

Dr Digby was still talking.

'The Best Minister's declared this an emergency,' he continued. 'He wants you found and dealt with. There's no getting away from him. He's putting everyone else you've had contact with into quarantine to stop the Pirus spreading.'

Alice shivered. The Best Minister for Everything Nicely Perfect again. Her insides knotted every time she heard his name.

'The Best Minister's becoming the most important man in the country. Lately he even tells the Prime Minster what to do. Be careful, he's very dangerous,' warned Dr Diana.

'What will he do with me?'

'Hopefully just lock you up so you don't spread the Pirus to everyone. But it could be worse, much worse. He thinks your Pirus could destroy us all,' said Dr Digby anxiously.

There was a silence while everyone stared at Alice. Suddenly feeling wobbly, she collapsed backwards into the soft armchair.

'Is Alice the first person to get this Pirus?' asked Jago curiously.

'She's the only person to have had a Pirus for decades.'

'How can that happen? Where do Piruses come from?'

Dr Digby's face lit up. 'Well, let me tell you about the mysterious habits of germs. I've got a brilliant slide show on it, would you like to see it?'

'No time, sorry!' Alice said quickly. Jago looked disappointed. 'How do you know I've truly got the Pirus?' Alice asked.

Dr Diana Goodish-Leech stared at her gravely. 'Because you've left a telltale trail of destruction behind you – worse than a hurricane. The doctor that visited and swabbed you, remember her?'

Alice nodded. 'She said I had a virus.'

'Yes, well, she was almost right: you had a Pirus and it looks like she's got it too. She's closed her surgery to humans and set up a sanctuary for insects. Says she's always had a passion for them. The whole building's now filled with spiders, ladybirds and beetles and attracts birds and frogs from miles around. She's very happy – but we think she'll never be normal again.'

'Spiders aren't insects,' muttered Jago, but no one was listening to him.

'It's nothing to do with me!' Alice felt really panicky now, she wanted to put her hands over her ears and shout at the doctors to stop talking. The trouble was that it all fitted together, the cold, the giggling, the animals . . . and it sounded like she was going to send everyone else crackers too.

'What about the antidote?' she asked hopefully. 'Do you know where it is?'

'I think there used to be one, but it's long-gone,' said Dr Diana, staring intently at Alice, almost as though she was weighing her up.

'What do you mean?' said Alice.

'It's disappeared. No one knows where it is.'

Alice's stomach twisted with disappointment. She hastily changed the subject.

'Will you report me to the Best Minister?'

Both doctors went white.

'Absolutely not!' said Dr Diana, horrified. 'We obey Public Health law on infections, not blindly do everything the Best Minister wants. If we reported you, I'd hate to think what he'd do to you.'

'I agree,' Dr Digby nodded. 'And if he finds out you've been here he'll put us in quarantine for ever – even though we've taken all the proper precautions to stop us catching your Pirus.'

Alice was relieved, but another concern struck her. 'Are my parents OK?'

'Well, there's an odd thing,' said Dr Digby. 'They've disappeared. The excellent Public Health nurses in Knott Sowell who went to put them into quarantine found your front door open, with nothing gone but your parents.'

'My mother's *gone*?' said Alice slowly, staring at her. She felt as though an ice cream snowball was sliding down her back. 'She can't have – she hasn't left the house since I was born. She's too afraid of catching germs!'

CHAPTER ELEVEN
The Secret Note

It was a long walk back to Tryton Mell.

After they had told Kevin what the Dr Goodish-Leeches had said, he and Jago kept shooting worried glances at Alice, but to her relief they didn't linger to discuss anything.

Instead, Jago marched them along at top speed.

'You're slowing down! If we're not there to meet Chloe on time, we're sunk!' he reminded them every few minutes.

'That's . . . coz . . . we're . . . dying . . .' panted Kevin, his face purple.

Alice didn't mind walking, she was glad of the time to think. What *had* happened to her parents? She didn't miss them, not at all, but she did hope that they were safe. Most of all though, she was now sure she had to take the antidote.

If I don't, someone's bound to notice that there's something odd about me and start investigating – then I'm in deep trouble, she thought, shuddering. She was still having nightmares about that transparent person-shaped box that the Best Minister's men had carried at her house.

'Perhaps I shouldn't go back,' she said aloud. 'They're sure to work out who I am soon. And if you haven't already got my Pirus, I don't want you catching it. Maybe I should look for the antidote instead.'

Jago shook his head firmly. 'No – Tryton Mell's the safest place for you right now. And if the Pirus is that catching, we're already infected. Anyway, where would you go? We've no idea where to find the antidote.'

Alice sighed with relief. Jago was right. She didn't have a clue where to start looking and the thought of running away was terrifying. *But going back is dangerous too,* she thought uneasily.

Then Jago made her feel a whole lot worse.

'I really think the Best Minister means to kill you if he finds you. It's the only logical thing to do.'

Alice shivered. She didn't think the Best Minister would go that far. But remembering the expression on the doctors' faces when they talked about him terrified her. Perhaps Jago was right.

Luckily, getting back in to Tryton Mell proved a lot easier than getting out. Chloe met them with squeaks of relief.

'You're late! I was really worried! Don't you realize it's only two hours till the bell rings?'

'Were we missed?' asked Alice anxiously.

'No, but you need to get to bed NOW!' Chloe hissed. 'Miss Grammaticus is prowling and she'll be along here again shortly!'

This made them flee to their dormitories at once.

The next morning, Alice frantically scrambled into her brown uniform as Nibbles contentedly curled up in her blazer pocket. Bravely ignoring him, Chloe quickly plaited one side of Alice's hair.

Emerald tackled the other.

'I know you and Chloe slipped out last night,' Emerald whispered into Alice's ear. 'But don't tell me anything, OK? That way I can't get you into trouble. But be careful, the others have been asking questions. They think there's something very odd about you.'

Alice looked down at the floor, cold dread rising over her. How long could she really stay hidden?

'And don't forget to put your pyjamas down the laundry chute!' instructed Emerald as she went to check on the others.

All clothes worn every day had to go down the chute; a new set of perfectly pressed pyjamas and crisply clean uniform mysteriously appeared each evening. Alice had noticed that hers were now neatly inscribed with 'Portland Maggott – Average' on name tags inside.

Alice picked up her pyjamas to sort them.

'What on earth . . ?'

A folded piece of paper fell out of her pyjama pocket and fluttered to the floor.

Alice looked at it. None of them usually put anything in their pockets; Mrs Peasley inspected them daily, punishing pupils if she found used tissues or other nasties.

She looked at Chloe, puzzled.

'It's not mine.'

'Open it!' said Chloe excitedly, peering over Alice's shoulder.

Alice unfolded it with shaking fingers. Inside was writing, all in old-fashioned italic letters. With increasing bewilderment, Alice read the words aloud.

Extra spellings for Portland Maggott — Average

1. *MOOD*
2. *FOE*
3. *GAS*
4. *SAP*

Study these words closely, as you need to take this test urgently. Be brave and obedient; you can't afford to make mistakes. Remember, if you don't know the answer you should say nothing.

The very best of luck to you, Portland Maggott.

Chloe stared at Alice.

'What on earth . . .'

'This must be a mistake – my spelling's not that

bad!' protested Alice hotly.

'No, I didn't mean that, it's just . . .' Chloe peered at the note closely. 'What a strange spelling list. I've never seen anything like this before in Tryton Mell.'

She looked up at Alice with anxious eyes.

'Do . . . do you think someone's trying to send you a secret message?'

'But who would do that?' Alice asked, bewildered.

'And what does it *mean*?' Chloe wondered, staring at it.

'It could be from them doctors,' said Kevin doubtfully, scrutinizing the note as they waited for lessons to start.

'It can't be; they didn't come near me,' said Alice. 'And I didn't check my pocket when I put my top on, that note might have been in there since yesterday.'

'Mrs Peasley does line up racks of fresh pyjamas downstairs for each dormitory every day,' mused Jago.

'Yeah, it would be easy to get to them without being spotted,' added Chloe.

Alice nodded in agreement. 'My name's on my

pyjamas – anyone could have put that note in my pocket.'

'What's it trying to tell us?' Chloe asked.

'That's what we need to find out. But first . . .' Jago pulled out his notebook. As Alice watched, he put a big tick next to number one on his list: Find out about the Pirus.

'We're making good progress, we've done a third of our tasks already.'

The other three rolled their eyes as Jago snapped his notebook shut.

Not a moment too soon.

'What are you noxious nitwits hanging about here for?' Mrs Peasley had a face like thunder. 'Averages – move it! Grab your hard hats and go to Explosive Equations now!'

They puzzled over the note between lessons all morning, but even Jago was stumped.

'It's no use. I've been through every code in the Dusty Side's best code-breaking books, even the top secret ones, but nothing works.'

'It must be easier than that,' said Alice. 'Whoever wrote it must've thought I could figure it out alone.'

But the note was the least of her worries. As they

slid across the slippery entrance hall on the way to lunch, Kevin stopped so suddenly that Alice fell over him.

'Look!' he hissed, pointing.

Alice's stomach plummeted.

Miss Grammaticus and Mrs Peasley were huddled together in front of the giant fireplace, heads bent over two very familiar red-tinged sheets of paper.

'ALICE DENT – DANGEROUS AND DEADLY!' Mrs Peasley read the heading aloud.

Alice went cold. Beside her, Chloe gasped, horrified.

'Well, she's not here. I'd have spotted the little twerp at once,' declared Miss Grammaticus.

'So would I,' agreed Mrs Peasley, with a self-satisfied nod. 'Still, it can't hurt to put this picture up all over, so that everyone knows what the grimy terror looks like.'

And then to Alice's horror, she looked up.

'MAGGOTT! What are you doing hanging—?'

Alice didn't wait to respond, she turned and fled down the main corridor, unfortunately bumping straight into Trugg and the other Perfect Poppets.

'Oy! Watch it, Maggott-breath!' Grabbing

Alice's arm, Trugg twisted it painfully behind her back, then shoved her so roughly that she fell sprawling across the hard floor.

The rest of the Poppets jeered.

Alice lay helpless and furious, her knees throbbing. She could feel Nibbles quivering in her pocket. Any second now Trugg would spot him . . .

'What on earth's going on here?'

'Nothing, sir!' said Trugg and Alice in unison; the Perfect Poppets scattering as Mr Pye approached.

But Alice had had enough.

'Right, that's it! We've got to crack that message right now, or I'm running away anyway!' she raged as Jago, Kevin and Chloe marched her firmly away. 'I can't stay here; if Trugg doesn't kill me first, someone's bound to work out who I am!'

'Shhh! You're attracting attention!' warned Jago, looking uneasily over his shoulder.

At this, Alice blew up completely. 'Look, I've got a Pirus, I'm very infectious, I'm going to get happiness, which apparently is the most dangerous thing going, I can't stop giggling but it probably doesn't matter coz I'm going to be suffocated by a massive pile of lovesick animals. Oh and did I mention that

the most dangerous man in the country is person-
ally HUNTING ME DOWN AND POSTING
UP MY PICTURE EVERYWHERE!'

'OK, OK – keep yer hair on!' Kevin backed away.

'It's all right,' said Chloe soothingly, glaring at
him and patting Alice on her arm. 'Come on, let's
get you cleaned up.'

'Yeah, it's a good thing yer can't see yerself in a
mirror, yer look a fright,' grinned Kevin. He
ducked, expecting Alice to go for him.

But she didn't.

Instead she stopped still and stared into space,
her eyes unfocusing.

'Mirror . . . mirror . . .' she muttered. 'I think . . .
give me that note!'

Hastily, Chloe pulled the folded paper out of her
pocket. Alice snatched it, studying the words whilst
the others watched, bemused.

'Oh . . . I thought it might be mirror-writing, but
it's not,' she said, shaking her head in disappointment. 'You know, like back to front . . .' Alice trailed
off abruptly, noticing that 'MOOD' backwards
spelt 'DOOM'.

'Jago, say the spelling words backwards!' she
demanded, her voice shaking with excitement.

'Pas . . . sag . . . eof . . . doom . . .' said Jago obediently.

Then as Alice gasped, Jago got it too.

'Pas . . . Passage of Doom!'

And as they all stared at each other in shock, Chloe said exactly what Alice was thinking.

'This must be a secret message, telling you to go down the Passage of Doom!'

'Excellent! Let's go NOW!' Kevin said, but Chloe shook her head unhappily.

'We can't,' she whispered. 'Mrs Peasley blew up the entrance before she sealed it off.'

'Why?' Alice and Kevin stared at her.

'The Passage of Doom was horrible, all dark and wet, so Mrs Peasley threw in dynamite to get rid of the damp smell. The entrance is completely blocked now.'

'And the message could be a trap. Whoever sent it might be trying to get rid of Alice,' warned Jago.

'I'm doomed anyway so I'll risk it, thank you,' Alice retorted, and Jago had no answer to that.

'So *how* do we get in?' asked Kevin.

Jago and Chloe looked at each other.

'No idea.' Chloe shrugged her shoulders.

This was bad news. There was silence whilst they

all thought.

'What about digging the rubble out?' Kevin suggested.

'Don't be silly,' Jago replied witheringly.

It was a long time before anyone else spoke. Then Alice had a sudden inspiration.

'What about the old library?' she asked. 'You told me we could get to anywhere from there.'

'I've never seen an entrance for it in the Dusty Side,' Jago said slowly. 'But there are dozens of doors; it's possible that we just haven't found it.'

'Let's go and look – we can sneak back to the fireplace now!' said Kevin eagerly. 'Then we can go down the Passage of Doom with yer, Alice.'

'You'll come with me?' Alice said, hardly daring to hope. She had been dreading going alone. 'It'll be really dangerous and if we're caught . . .'

'We'll risk it,' said Jago.

'Of course we're coming with you,' Chloe said indignantly. 'We're friends, remember?'

And in spite of everything, this made Alice glow inside.

'Meet yer there!' shouted Kevin. 'I'll be back in a min!'

'Where are you going?' asked Chloe.

'To get pyjamas for yer all of course. We ain't going to get far in our blazers!'

They had a nasty shock when they crept into the entrance hall. Mrs Peasley stood by the fireplace, humming as she stapled up a massive picture of Alice.

Luckily Kevin reacted before anyone could panic.

'Give me Nibbles!' he demanded, and after Alice had reluctantly dug the protesting mouse out of her pocket, Kevin snuck around to the telephone box and let him go.

'AAAARGH!'

Mrs Peasley screeched – Nibbles had scrabbled straight over her foot.

'YOU PESKY VARMINT! Now where's my MOUSE 'N' LOUSE KILL?' Muttering, Mrs Peasley disappeared into her office as Nibbles scuttled into Alice's hand, quivering.

'CLIMB!' Kevin hissed, sprinting back, and they all piled into the chimney.

Alice's heart sank as she climbed out into the library. Everywhere she looked were odd little doors, dozens of them, nestling in between shelves crammed with books.

Jago took charge.

'We'll take a wall each – check each label, but hurry!'

Silence fell. As the minutes passed, Alice scanned labels with increasing desperation.

'It's not here, we've checked every door,' said Jago after they had searched for an hour. He sank down on to the sofa.

'We can't give up now!' protested Chloe.

But Jago had just said what they were all thinking.

'We've got to think like Professor Tryton . . .' Chloe screwed up her eyes.

'Forget it, we're dead!' said Kevin gloomily, throwing himself down on a sofa. In the end, only Chloe continued to prowl around, still searching.

'Leave it, Chloe,' Jago instructed her. 'The entrance to the Passage of Doom isn't here.'

But for once Jago was wrong.

'Hey, I've got an idea!' Chloe shrieked suddenly, running over to the horror section of the library. She began to pull the books off the shelves frantically.

'Are yer off yer rocker?' asked Kevin.

'No … it's got to be … yes, here it is!'

The other three jumped up eagerly and crowded round to see. Behind a stack of loose shelves, hidden by rows of horror books, was a coffin-shaped door. Over the top of it was an untidy inscription in blood red letters:

Prepare To Meet Yor Doom

They had found the door to the Passage of Doom at last.

CHAPTER TWELVE
The Passage of Doom

'**L**et's go!' said Jago, reaching forward.

But the other three stood frozen.

'Aren't you scared?' asked Alice, surprised. She was terrified.

'Nah, I'm not scared of anyone who can't spell properly,' shrugged Jago. 'Everyone knows that "your" is spelt Y-O-U-R, not Y-O-R.' And he pushed the door wide open before they could stop him.

Alice and Chloe backed away, coughing as a damp, dank smell hit them, but the boys didn't seem to notice.

'It's blacker than a black hole!' Kevin exclaimed, peering into the shaft.

'Nothing's blacker than a black hole,' Jago said severely.

Kevin ignored him. He had spotted something.

'Look – that's the way down!'

Alice saw it too, a line of metal pegs leading downwards, glinting in the light they had let in.

'No way!' Chloe drew back. She wasn't good with heights.

'Well you can't stay here. Miss Grammaticus will lock you up for ever. But first she'll torture you until you tell her where we've gone, and you're bound to tell her about Alice,' said Jago.

Chloe went white.

'I guess I'm coming with you then.'

'Good because I'd have dragged you along otherwise.'

'I can't see anything,' Alice said, hastily interrupting as Chloe glared at Jago.

'Got it sorted.' Kevin pulled out candles and a box of matches with a flourish.

'Wow – good thinking!' said Alice, seriously impressed.

They had an anxious moment when the metal pegs ended – high above the tunnel floor.

'We'll have to jump, but it means we can't come back this way,' said Jago, looking up at the coffin-shaped light that shone through the doorway high above them.

'Well let's hope we can get out the other end then,' retorted Alice.

'Yeah, and for goodness' sake be careful, I don't know what we'll do if anyone breaks a leg.' Chloe as usual was worrying, but she didn't need to, they all landed safely on the rocky floor beneath.

I'm not scared, Alice repeated to herself as they hurried along, breathing in the sour air. Her school shoes slipped on the slimy floor; it was getting wetter as the tunnel got narrower.

'That's odd, Tryton Mell's on high ground – so surely we should be going downhill by now,' Jago observed.

The others didn't reply.

Time passed. Alice's feet were freezing. She began to wonder if they would be trapped down there for ever. But luckily, before she got frostbite,

Jago made them stop.

'What's that?'

They all stared too.

In the middle of the tunnel was a red painted door.

It was a very ordinary door, just like any front door on any house. Under the white bell push was a sign that said 'Ring me'.

'That's odd,' said Chloe.

The door didn't block their way. There were gaps on either side large enough for them to walk past. They could easily go on and ignore it.

But somehow they didn't seem able to do that.

Kevin reached out for the bell.

'Wait, we could just go around it.' Chloe said.

Alice shook her head. 'I don't think we're supposed to do that, I think this is some sort of test.'

'Or a trap,' muttered Chloe.

'What about opening it?' Kevin tried the door handle instead. It was locked.

'Why don't we do what it says and ring the bell?' Alice asked.

'Better not,' said Chloe nervously. 'You never know what you might wake up. In every story I've ever read it's never been a good idea to ring a random bell.'

Alice looked at them all, fighting an urge to giggle. The odd door was setting her off again.

'Let's vote on it,' she said. 'I'm for ringing it.'

'And me!' added Kevin cheerfully, 'but I don't expect nothin'.'

'I don't want to,' said Chloe. 'Haven't any of you ever read *Alice's Adventures in Wonderland*? That's full of labels telling her to do stuff and terrible things happen!'

'Yeah, but she were OK in the end,' retorted Kevin.

'That's coz it's a book, you can get anyone out of trouble in a story. This is real life, Kevin.'

'Jago?' asked Alice. 'What do you think?'

Jago went to inspect the door from the other side. 'We have to ring it,' he said at last. 'If we don't then we'll never know whether we were supposed to. We'll always be wondering about it.'

'Oh no!' said Chloe faintly. 'This is always what gets people into trouble in books.'

'I'll do it!' Kevin pressed the button before anyone could stop him. A sharp ringing filled the tunnel.

Then there was silence.

'See . . . nothin' happened,' said Kevin triumphantly.

A second later the ground beneath him gave way and he plunged downwards.

Chloe screamed.

'What the . . .?'

They ran to the spot where Kevin had disappeared. There was nothing to see. The stone slab had righted itself. When Jago cautiously tested it, there was no movement.

'It's as solid as . . . well, as solid as rock I suppose. Look, you can see the edges. Anyone ringing the bell would have to stand on it. I wonder—'

'We have to help Kevin right now!' interrupted Alice, stepping forward and pressing the bell.

Even though she expected it, falling through the floor almost made Alice's heart stop.

Please don't hurt too much! she begged silently as she plummeted.

But it didn't hurt. Instead she landed on something squishy and pink. As she lay there, blinking in the dazzling artificial light and waiting for her stomach to catch up, Alice heard the best sound ever – Kevin's voice.

'Yer made it then!' he said, smiling, his brown

hair wild and dirt smudged all across his cheeks.

'Wha . . . where . . .?' As Alice stuttered, Kevin grabbed her hand and pulled her to her feet. To her surprise, apart from the giant pink inflatable she'd just fallen on, and the fact they seemed to be underground, the room looked like a normal kitchen.

A familiar sharp ringing sounded overhead.

'Not again! How many of you pesky kids are there?'

Alice turned, startled. Kevin grinned.

'Portland Maggott, meet Yor Doom!' he announced. 'Her name's Yorlanda, but she's called Yor for short.'

Alice stared at Yorlanda Doom. Yorlanda stared back. Yorlanda was tiny, with white hair and a lived-in face, but there were lines of steel in her frown. Alice felt a little scared of her.

Then Chloe fell through the ceiling and hit the inflatable.

'I'll put the kettle on then; three mugs of tea coming up.'

'Could we have four please? Jago will be down in a minute,' said Chloe, scrambling down shakily from the giant pink cushion.

Within ten minutes they were all sitting around

the kitchen table eating chocolate chip cookies and drinking hot tea.

'Good for shock,' Yorlanda Doom insisted, scrutinizing them all as they drank.

'Please – who are you? Where are we? And what's with the door?' The questions burst out of Alice.

Yorlanda Doom chuckled. 'Well, let's see – many years ago I was the librarian at Tryton Mell, but this is my home now. The Passage of Doom and the red door were rather nifty ideas of my dear friend Professor Tryton. He guessed there might be a need one day for a secret way out of Tryton Mell for pupils. So he asked me to help and made the Passage so frightening that only brave children who were desperate, or who had been told to, would dare enter.'

'So that's why there's lots of scary rumours about it,' said Chloe, her dark eyes wide.

'But why the door?' asked Jago. 'Isn't it unnecessary? Can't the Passage get you straight here?'

Alice looked at Jago. He was as neat as if he'd just come down to breakfast, his face cleanly scrubbed and not a black hair out of place. How did he manage it?

'Ah yes, the door. If the Passage led straight here, the bad guys would come here too. So the Professor created the door to protect both me and anyone running away from them. He said that people who were brave and adventurous or just plain curious would ring the bell, but dull boring people wouldn't bother. He guessed that any children escaping down the Passage of Doom would have those qualities and ring it, hoping it might help them, but any grown-ups chasing them would likely ignore it.'

'I wouldn't have rung it if the others hadn't first,' muttered Chloe.

'Ah but you did, didn't you?' said Yorlanda Doom. 'Too scared to ring it for yourself but brave enough to ring it to save your friends. That proves the Professor was right.'

'Where does the Passage end up?' asked Jago, as Chloe tried to get over the shock of being called brave.

Yorlanda Doom smiled. 'In the local sewage works of course. Now, which one of you is Portland Maggott? I've been given this envelope to give to you.'

With the others watching curiously, Alice took the fat envelope and tore it open. Inside were pages of detailed directions, written in neat black capitals.

'Who are they from?' Alice asked as she sifted through the sheets, puzzled. 'Will they take us to the Pirus antidote?'

'They're from another of the Professor's friends. These are dangerous times, so it's better that you don't know too much. If you follow these correctly and don't get caught, you'll meet his friend yourself. Now, one more thing.'

Yorlanda handed Alice a small silver key. 'You might need this in an emergency, so don't lose it.'

Alice turned the key over in her hands.

'What's it for?' she asked curiously. Yorlanda Doom leant forward.

'It gets you into the Toilet Tendering Service – they'll help you if you're in trouble. Nearly every public toilet block's part of it, even those inside buildings and shops. Look for a locked door that's never open – a door that no one ever thinks about – and use the key. Once you've opened that door, you can ask for any help you need.' She then gave them exact instructions on what to do.

As the four of them listened, their eyes widened in astonishment. Alice couldn't help it, she dissolved into helpless giggles.

'Yer joking – right?' asked Kevin.

'I never joke about important things,' said Yorlanda, looking offended. 'Right, two more things: firstly, make sure no one follows you. Secondly, remember this: if you don't know the answer, you should say nothing.'

Alice stared at her. *That's what it had said on the spelling list too.* She opened her mouth to ask another question, but Yorlanda Doom shook her head firmly.

'No more questions, time is of the essence. Off you go – I need to get up to the secret and amazing things that I do daily. Luckily the neighbours suspect nothing; that's the beauty of being my age and living in a semi-detached house.'

She opened the front door and pushed them out on to the porch.

From the front, Alice could see that the house was unremarkable; almost exactly like all the others in the leafy green road. Only the kitchen was underground, built into the hillside so that the Passage of Doom could drop into it.

Alice thought that Yorlanda's secrets were safe; nobody would ever guess what was inside such a boring looking house.

'Look in the shed down there; you might find

something useful. I don't use it now the boys have grown up,' Yorlanda Doom called after them, pointing to the side passage.

She was partly right. There *was* something in the shed. Whether it was useful or not was another question entirely.

CHAPTER THIRTEEN
Saltley Rockpool

'What on earth is it?' asked Alice.

'A quadracycle!' said Kevin in delight, as he tugged the battered blue four-seater bicycle out of the shed.

'Technically it's a quad tandem,' corrected Jago.

'This is gonna be fun!' Kevin hoisted the machine upright and inspected it, turning pedals and checking chains. 'It looks in good nick too.'

'I'll go in front,' said Jago. 'You need to be good at

physics to steer this thing.'

'No way mate,' Kevin replied firmly. 'I'm the best biker in town, I'm in front.' He seized the front handlebars and swung his leg over the crossbar.

Alice sighed. They would argue all day if she didn't step in.

'You go on the back,' she told Jago. 'I can't ride a bike, so I'll be all over the place. You'll need your physics skills to make up for me. Also, you're our best code-breaker; it'll need an expert to work out these directions. Let Kevin steer and you tell him where to go.'

'OK,' said Jago, mollified, taking the directions from her and scanning them closely. They waited impatiently as he jotted notes on the pages.

'Hurry up!' urged Alice. She was having trouble with a flock of sparrows perching on her cycle helmet. Nibbles scolded them with sharp squeaks.

'I'm ready.' Jago climbed neatly on to the back of the tandem.

'Which way, mate?'

'And where are we going?' asked Chloe eagerly.

'Turn left here. My calculations suggest we're going to the seaside, to a town called Saltley Rockpool,' he told them as they wobbled down the road.

This wasn't the answer Alice expected, but a big grin spread over her face.

'Oh wow! I've never been to the seaside!'

'What? You've never seen the sea?' asked Chloe in surprise.

Alice shook her head.

'I'll tell yer what!' Kevin's eyes lit up. 'Let's have a day on the beach – I'll take yer surfing and rock-pooling, and teach yer to build sandcastles—'

'Kevin!' Jago interrupted crossly. 'We've got a job to do.'

'Oh, all right, spoilsport.' Kevin looked as disappointed as Alice felt.

By the time they had fallen off three times, they were all fed up with the quad tandem. It just wasn't very good at going around corners or up and down hills. This was unfortunate as the directions took them mostly through twisty little lanes and across bumpy fields.

'If we have to go much further, let's ditch the bike and walk,' suggested Alice, groaning in pain as they took a hump-backed bridge too fast and she fell off.

'It's OK – yer softies don't need to do that coz we're here!' Kevin told them, grinning.

He was right. They had reached a sign that read, 'Welcome to Saltley Rockpool'.

'Is that noise the sea?' Alice asked eagerly, listening as they stopped. Excited giggles bubbled up inside her. She was going to see the sea!

'Of course it is. If yer hurry up and find Professor Tryton's friend we might have time to build sandcastles,' said Kevin, full of enthusiasm.

'Well, we just need to work out what ninety-one round stones means, and then we're done,' Jago told them, frowning at the sheet of paper in his hand.

'What – don't you know where we're going?' Alice abruptly stopped giggling.

'No, this last bit's a clue that we have to solve. "Find ninety-one round stones, and you'll find me," that's all it says.'

'For goodness' sake! Why can't they just tell us where to go? Why are they making it so hard?' Chloe was getting crosser by the minute.

'They can't take the risk,' Alice told her. 'What if we got caught and the Best Minister got hold of these directions?'

'Yeah, or if we was captured and tortured on the way?' added Kevin. 'This way we can't tell them nothin' coz we don't know nothin' until we get there.'

'We really won't know anything if you don't hurry up,' Jago told him impatiently.

Saltley Rockpool was the sort of town that explained why Mrs Dent had always refused to let Alice go on school trips to the seaside.

'Think of all those people from everywhere mixing and passing on their local germs, let alone the terrible diseases you'll catch from paddling in the sea,' she would say, horrified, when Alice begged to go.

Despite these warnings, Alice beamed with delight as they walked into the town. Even though it was getting dark, the little shops were still packed with families, many happily licking ice creams.

'Follow me,' Jago ordered, turning into the main street.

Alice hurried after him. Part of her still worried that they weren't sure what to do next, but mostly she skipped inside with joy. She thought about running along the beach without shoes, wondering what sand would feel like between her toes.

Chloe was the first to notice something odd.

'Err . . . Alice . . . that camera . . . I think it's following you.'

Alice whirled round.

'You're joking!' Alarmed, she stared up at the camera, which was mounted high up on a narrow pole. Too late she realized that this was a very bad move; she was now clearly showing her face to it.

'Chloe! Kevin! HIDE!' Jago instructed hastily, sliding himself into a nearby doorway. Kevin pulled Chloe back, all three of them out of range of the lens.

Alice was the only one it could see.

She experimented by walking on down the brightly lit street. The camera followed her, revolving silently on its little platform.

'I think they've found me,' she announced unnecessarily.

She was kicking herself. After everything that had happened that day, her hair was now a complete mess and she looked more like the Alice Dent on the posters. If only she had kept her hair neatly in plaits. She might not have been recognized, not as Alice Dent, anyway. And the Best Minister wouldn't care less about trying to find a missing Portland Maggott.

'Let's get off this street,' said Kevin urgently, and they dived into a narrow side passage, hidden from the camera.

'You've been spotted. The Best Minister's men will be coming for you. What do we do now?' asked Jago.

'Keep moving.' Alice couldn't see what else they could do. 'We have to find Professor Tryton's friend – and hope they help protect me from the Best Minister.'

'Let's hope his friend knows where to find the antidote too, otherwise you're in real trouble.'

They darted through the streets, dodging the cameras and staying in the shadows. Twice, police cars whooshed by. Alice's heart almost stopped, but they didn't spot her.

'Do you know anything about ninety-one round stones?' they asked passers-by, but no one knew anything.

'This is silly,' said Alice at last, as they reached the road that led to the harbour. 'We can't stumble round hoping to come across it; the police are going to find me before then. I'm sure Professor Tryton's friend must think I can work it out. They wouldn't leave it to chance.'

'There's a street map on that wall, let's look at that for clues,' said Jago, pointing. He nearly got flattened as they all rushed over.

'There's nothing obvious here,' said Chloe. 'Harbour, a beach, shops . . .'

'Look at the railway station – it's humungous!' interrupted Kevin. Jago peered over his shoulder.

'That's odd; it's much too big for a town this size. Perhaps it's Victorian, everyone travelled by train then.'

'I love trains!' Kevin perked up.

'Hang on,' said Alice, 'what's this?' She pointed to a small circle at the end of the long harbour wall.

'A lighthouse,' said Chloe. 'Disused since 1991,' she added, peering at the tiny label.

'A lighthouse,' said Alice slowly. 'Are lighthouses made out of round stones?'

'Hey, I think you've got it!' said Jago. For once he looked impressed. 'Come on, let's find out.'

But it was too late.

They were going to be caught: a bank of blue lights swept towards them from nearly every direction.

They stared at each other, Chloe pale with panic. But strangely, now that things looked so hopeless, Alice felt calm. Perhaps this was part of the Pirus effect.

'I'm not giving up now!'

'Get on with it then,' urged Kevin. 'I'll stay 'ere; try and delay them. I'll tell 'em I saw someone climbing up the cliffs.'

'We'd better all stay,' said Jago. 'Spread out and point in different directions, that will help.'

'Can yer lie?' asked Kevin, really interested to know.

'Not well, but I can roughly calculate for them the theoretical probabilities of someone choosing a route based on available topographical data. That should confuse the average person,' said Jago, almost smiling.

Within minutes of leaving the others, Alice had reached the lighthouse. *Too dark to see the sea now,* she thought sadly, as the moon disappeared behind clouds. She ran up the steps, feeling very alone.

It was cold on the exposed staircase. Alice looked over at the blackness of the water. There was an odd fishy sort of smell about it, and she tasted salt on the gusts of wind.

Alice shivered. She had never imagined that the seaside could be so scary.

Close to, the lighthouse was like a big black

nightmare leering over her, made worse by the crashing waves. Alice took a deep breath, jumped up to the impressive front door and knocked loudly.

A small peephole flipped open.

'There's a bath of red chilli sauce above you,' said a stern voice. 'If you don't give me the password immediately, you'll be dyed blood-red, all ready for Halloween.'

What password? Alice wondered in panic. Dyeing was not an option, not if she could help it.

'I don't know the password – but please let me in, I need to find Professor Tryton's friend!' she pleaded, feeling seriously frightened now. This certainly wasn't going to plan.

'No password, no entry. You might be an imposter,' the stern voice told her.

Miserably, Alice turned away from the door. The sirens had almost reached the harbour. It was too late to ask the others for help. She was doomed.

CHAPTER FOURTEEN
Professor Tryton's Friend

It was only after she had jumped down four steps that Alice realized that she had known the password all along.

'It's NOTHING!' she shouted, running back and banging furiously on the door. 'The password's nothing!'

And, almost as if it was word activated, the heavy door swung open.

Alice stared.

She had expected Professor Tryton's friend to be, well, slightly odd, but this woman looked completely in charge and totally normal. (Well, as normal as anyone dressed in bright orange waterproofs could look.) Yes, she was unremarkable except for her vivid blue eyes.

The woman smiled. 'Come in! I was seriously worried there; I thought Yor Doom had failed to give you the password.'

'No, she did tell me, but I almost didn't get it. "If you don't know the answer, you should say nothing . . ."' Alice explained, thinking of the cryptic words in the mysterious spelling list and Yorlanda Doom's instructions.

She stepped into the little round room, looking around with interest. The only thing in it was a magnificent metal staircase that spiralled through from floor to ceiling.

'Please, who are you? And why are you helping me?'

'I'm Principal Swift. Like Yor Doom, I'm another of Professor Tryton's friends. We're all trying to stop the Best Minister from being even more horrible to children than he is now.' The Principal smiled again. 'And you must be Portland Maggott – or should I say Alice Dent? I've been expecting you. You've come for the antidote, I presume?'

'Y-Yes – you know who I really am?'

'Of course I do. What child apart from Alice Dent or a lookalike imposter sent by the Best Minister would be hunting for the antidote?'

'Do . . . do you know where it is?'

'We've been looking for the antidote ever since we first heard about you. The only vial left went missing a long time ago, but luckily we headteachers are excellent at tracking down lost things – we have to do it every day in school. We think we've found it—'

'Where . . ?' Alice interrupted eagerly.

Principal Swift frowned at the interruption.

Alice fell silent immediately. She guessed the Principal's pupils behaved perfectly for her in school just because they wanted to – she was that kind of teacher.

'Do you know what's special about Saltley Rock-pool, Alice?'

'Best cream teas in the world?' Alice had read this on the welcome sign.

'Good try, but even better than that.'

'Best beaches in Britain?' This had been on the tourist information board.

'No, something much better.'

Alice shrugged her shoulders.

'It's got the Lost Property Office for the whole rail network of the United Kingdom. Everything lost on a train ends up here, so that's where the antidote is – in the Lost Property Office.'

'How do you know that?'

'We know it got lost on the way to the Just in Case Place after the last Pirus epidemic.'

'The *what*?'

'Just in Case Place. It's where those in charge put things that might be needed one day,' explained Principal Swift. 'It got lost on the train going there, so it's bound to be in lost property. Well, to be fair, it was more that the train got lost.'

'Trains don't get lost!' protested Alice.

'Happens all the time, you're waiting for a train and it doesn't arrive. That's because it's got lost.'

'That's coz it's been cancelled!'

'That's what they tell you. So what are you going to do with the antidote, Alice – take it?'

Alice nodded. That had seemed the best thing to do in Tryton Mell, what with the animals sticking to her and the giggling attacks. She had been so afraid that they would put her in danger of being discovered and reported to the Best Minister.

But now she wasn't so sure.

She slipped a hand inside her pocket and stroked Nibbles. *I'll miss you if I get rid of the Pirus,* she thought sadly.

'We'll help you, whatever you choose to do,' said Principal Swift, considering Alice with those eyes again. Alice squirmed under her intense gaze.

'But if you use the antidote, Alice, you'll never get a Pirus like this again. And if you give the antidote to your friends they won't get the Pirus either. Is that really what you want?'

Alice stared at her dumbly. *I don't know!* she thought, gulping hard.

'The Best Minister's determined to get the antidote too. He'll use it to protect himself and then he'll copy it and force everyone to take it. This Pirus will be eliminated, which means there'll be nothing left to stop the Best Minister carrying out his evil plans. He's scared of truly happy people; they can't be frightened into doing bad things and won't co-operate in his nasty little schemes.'

Alice stared. She'd never thought about it like that before.

'So I advise you *not* to take the antidote, but find

and destroy it so the Best Minister can't use it,' the Principal continued. 'Do you understand what I'm saying, Alice?'

Alice nodded slowly, thinking. *If I take the antidote I'll be safe, but I'll lose Nibbles and the Best Minister will win. But if I destroy it instead, I'll be in terrible danger – but I could stop the Best Minister doing more terrible things.*

She thought that Principal Swift was an excellent headteacher all right, offering you a choice but in a way that there really was no choice.

'OK, I won't take the antidote; I'll destroy it instead,' she said, making up her mind at last.

'Excellent! Then there's one more thing. After you've destroyed the antidote, you must find out exactly what the Best Minister's plans are and stop him carrying them out.'

Alice stared at her, speechless with shock.

'Do you understand, Alice? You must stop him!'

'Wha-What do you mean?'

'We know he's made big plans for something in the next couple of days. All Professor Tryton's friends have been trying to find out what these are, but the only thing we're certain about is that your headmistress is involved. That's why you need to do this, Alice, you're the only one who can get near her to find out the plans and stop the Best Minister in time.'

'Miss Grammaticus? Are you sure?' Alice gasped, flabbergasted.

Principal Swift nodded.

'So . . . so I have to go back to Tryton Mell?'

'I'm afraid so – oh dear! Look! We're out of time, the police are upon us. You need to go. I'll stay here and stop them catching you or we're finished.'

Alice looked out of the window. The blue sirens had reached the harbour.

'I led them straight here! I'm so sorry!' Cold horror trickled down her spine.

'It's OK; you didn't have much choice,' said Principal Swift kindly. 'Now forget that and focus. You need to stop the Best Minister. If you don't, we're all in great danger.'

'But I'm only eleven!' protested Alice.

'Eleven's plenty old enough to save the world. You've done brilliantly so far, I know you'll do it.'

A sudden thunderous thud interrupted them, making Alice jump.

'That's a battering ram!' said Principal Swift, steadying her. 'Right, we need to get you out right now! I'll stay here and delay them.'

'But . . .'

'Don't worry about me,' Principal Swift smiled. 'It's amazing what havoc I can create with a bunch of confiscated fireworks and a bit of chemistry-lesson-made explosive.'

She hurried Alice down the staircase and outside on to a narrow platform. By now the whole lighthouse was shaking. The Principal helped Alice into the small rowing boat that was moored to the platform and threw a pair of oars down to her.

'Row to the other side of the harbour wall!' she shouted. 'You'll be hidden there!' Before Alice could protest, Principal Swift had untied the rope and given the boat a hard shove.

'But I can't row!' Alice shrieked. She had never even been in a boat before. But the Principal had disappeared.

She was alone.

'Great, just great,' she muttered crossly and dipped the oars cautiously into the water. The boat swung around in a perfect circle.

By the time that Alice had got the hang of going forwards, the lighthouse was swarming with police.

She could see them clearly, black against the multi-coloured flashes and explosions.

It was very dark on the water. As she rowed, Alice thought about what Principal Swift had asked her to do. She imagined Jago making another list.

Find and destroy the antidote
Discover the Minister's plans
Stop him and save the world

Fear drenched her. How could she do any of that? She was only slightly cheered up by the friendly seals that escorted her all the way to the shore.

CHAPTER FIFTEEN
The Pirus Antidote

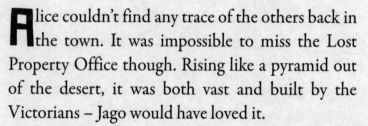

Alice couldn't find any trace of the others back in the town. It was impossible to miss the Lost Property Office though. Rising like a pyramid out of the desert, it was both vast and built by the Victorians – Jago would have loved it.

Alice rang the doorbell without much hope. It was now the middle of the night; surely it wouldn't be open.

She was wrong.

'Can I help you?' The attendant in blue overalls looked just like a sixth former from school, except that he was friendly.

'Yes, I need to find . . .' Alice trailed off. She realized that she had no idea what to say.

'We can search by name, by train taken, or by item, but that's harder. If it's an umbrella we've got one million, two hundred thousand and ninety six of them. Still, I've labelled them all,' the attendant said, beaming. Alice thought he'd get on well with Jago.

'Shall we start with your name?'

Alice shook her head. There was no way she could tell him that.

Over the next half hour, tapping hard on his computer, the Lost Property attendant took her through every search Alice could think of, even 'Pirus' and 'Antidote', but nothing came up.

'Wow, this is turning into a really exciting night!' His eyes gleamed. 'I love a challenge!'

'If you knew the name of the person who lost it, maybe you've already sent it back to them,' said Alice.

He shook his head.

'We never do that – think of the postage.' His eyes widened at the thought. 'If it's important enough to them they'll come and get it.'

'Maybe you've thrown it away.'

'No chance, we keep everything for ever – unless it bites or it's past its sell by date. Now don't despair, let's have some of my mum's home-made ginger beer and lemon puff biscuits, that always helps a search along.'

As they sat on a lost sofa munching biscuits, Alice thought that the attendant was possibly the happiest person she'd ever met. He certainly didn't need her Pirus.

'My name's Jonathon – I'm the Chief Apprentice here,' he told Alice proudly.

'How—' Alice stopped, alarmed.

Someone was coming into the Lost Property Office.

She could see reflections in the mirror, two tall men in black suits. Icy fear gripped her.

The Best Minister's men had arrived.

'Oh wonderful, more customers!' Jonathon looked only mildly surprised when Alice dived behind the sofa.

'Quickly, boy, find us the Pirus antidote – we

haven't got all day!' said one of the men impatiently.

'That's funny, I've never heard of a Pirus before tonight, then two . . .'

Alice jumped up, shaking her head frantically. She knew that she might be seen, but she had to stop Jonathon talking.

It worked.

'Oh, never mind, a Pirus you say? How do you spell that?' asked Jonathon, winking at her. Alice didn't have time to feel relief. She had to find the antidote, and find it fast, before the Best Minister's men found it. She slid through the door into the Lost Property store while their backs were still turned, then halted in shock.

It wasn't just that the room was vast, with aisles stretching into infinity, or that the shelves were crammed with every kind of object (how could anyone lose a helicopter on a train?). It was more the sheer impossibility of finding one tiny bottle of antidote in there.

Alice jogged down the aisles in despair. The objects were arranged by what they were or by people's names if they were named, and she scanned the labels as she passed.

Fall, Mrs A, False Body Parts, False teeth (this was

a big section), *Falstaff, J . . .*

The Best Minister's men were checking the aisles now too. This made Alice slow down. She was terrified of bumping into them.

'I've sent for a hundred extra men!' one called. 'We'll find it in no time then!'

Alice decided she definitely wasn't going to be there when enemy reinforcements arrived.

On a whim, she checked out Professor Tryton in the 'T' aisle. But it seemed that the only thing he'd lost on a train was a skipping rope.

She was jogging through the 'S' aisle when a label caught her eye:

Professor R. B. Snortle.

Alice stopped. She knew that name. And then she remembered clearly the Dr Goodish-Leeches telling her that Professor Snortle had discovered the Pirus.

If he discovered the Pirus, perhaps he discovered the antidote too, then left it on a train by mistake, thought Alice. With growing excitement, she lifted the small metal box off the shelf.

'Hey! You there!'

Alice jumped. *Oh no!* She'd been spotted!

The Best Minister's men were dashing towards

her. Clutching the box tightly, Alice sprinted down the long aisle. If she could just dive through the reception door, she could escape.

But it opened before she reached it.

Enemy reinforcements had arrived.

Alice skidded to a halt as a stream of black-suited figures poured through the reception door. Her heart thudded wildly – she was going to be caught!

'Grab her!'

Alice dived sideways, hugging Professor Snortle's box tightly to her chest, but she was trapped. Foot-steps were getting closer and closer . . .

'This way!' shrieked the Chief Apprentice, his head popping out of a hatch in the wall. Alice didn't hesitate. She leapt towards Jonathon and through the hatch, landing in a long, dark, damp-smelling corridor.

'Jump in! I'll push you!' Jonathon pointed to a small cart resting on miniature rails.

'It's how the lost property comes to us from the trains,' he explained, closing the hatch as Alice fell into the truck. 'It's your only way out!'

They could hear the shouts of the Best Minister's men, very close now. One of them tugged at the hatch.

'Hold on!' shouted Jonathon. He gave the cart a mighty shove, just as the Best Minister's men burst in.

'Stop her!' shrieked the closest man, but it was too late. The cart flew out of the door at the other end of the corridor and rattled along rails, high above the brightly lit platforms of Saltley Rockpool train station.

As it twisted and turned on the tracks, Alice had to cling on with one hand to avoid being thrown out. She clutched Professor Snortle's box tightly in her other hand.

Angry shouts suddenly erupted behind her. Alice turned. *Oh no!* Other carts were following her – men hanging off them, their feet dangling. If she wasn't as fast as lightning when she hit the ground they would catch her.

As the cart plummeted downwards, Alice scanned the station anxiously. Yes, there it was!

She had spotted exactly what she was looking for.

Even though she was braced for it, Alice still flew through the air head first when the little truck hit the buffers at the end of the line. Luckily, she landed just where she wanted to be – right outside the ladies' toilets on the station concourse.

She dived inside, desperately hoping that Yorlanda Doom had told her the truth about the Toilet Tendering Service. Otherwise she was finished.

'Watch the floor love, it's wet.' The cleaner moved her mop to let Alice pass – then skilfully twisted it sideways. 'Oi!' she yelled fiercely at the men chasing Alice. 'You can't come in here, it's the Ladies'!' The men skidded to a furious halt.

Alice jogged down the white-tiled corridor, grinning. Wrinkling her nose at the smell (she was beginning to understand why Mrs Dent freaked out about public toilets), she gasped in relief when she spotted an unremarkable locked door just like the one that Yorlanda Doom had told her to look for. Twenty seconds later she had opened it with Yorlanda Doom's key.

What she saw behind the door made her halt in surprise.

At the end of a narrow, well-lit passage, looking very out-of-place, was a brightly painted red-and-yellow cottage-style door, complete with a doormat and tubs of orange flowers.

After turning the key behind her, Alice stepped forwards. But before she knocked on the door,

Alice sat on the floor and opened the metal box. Lying snugly inside was a glass vial, filled with a clear liquid. Alice read the handwritten instructions on the lid.

'Two drops and you'll be back to normal. One drop for each close contact and they'll be protected.'

She had found the Pirus antidote.

CHAPTER SIXTEEN
The Best Minister's Plan

Alice gazed at the vial for a long time. It was made of glass; all she had to do was crush it to destroy the antidote. It was just that she couldn't bring herself to do it – not yet. At last, sighing, she slipped it inside her pyjama pocket. *I'll stamp on it if the Best Minister or his men get anywhere near me again,* she promised herself, knocking tentatively on the cottage door.

It was opened at once – by a woman who wore a frown, red overalls and yellow rubber gloves that exactly matched the door's colour scheme.

'What do you want?' she asked irritably.

Alice stared at her, jumpy with nerves. She remembered what Yorlanda Doom had told her to say, but it was going to sound incredibly silly.

'Hurry up, girl! I haven't got all day!'

'I claim use of the Toilet Tendering Service,' she whispered, really hoping that this wouldn't make the woman furious. But to her surprise, the woman immediately snapped to attention, all irritation gone now.

'What account?' she demanded, her voice military crisp.

'Professor Tryton's,' Alice told her, exactly as Yorlanda Doom had instructed.

The woman stood even straighter and saluted smartly.

'Toilet Tendering Service at your command. How can I help?'

Alice grinned with relief.

'I need a shower, hair bobbles, a brown tunic with scarlet trim and transport to Tryton Mell really soon please!'

'You'd better come in,' sighed the lady, pushing the door wide open.

It was Mrs Peasley who opened the front door of Tryton Mell.

'Ah, Portland Maggott! So you've decided to crawl back. Couldn't manage without your dimwit friends? Well don't worry, the police picked up the little numpties in Saltley Rockpool – they're safe in my office.'

Thank goodness they're OK, thought Alice, but she had a horrible feeling that Mrs Peasley's smirk when she said 'safe' hadn't boded well for the others.

'Yes, Mrs Peasley,' was all she replied though, standing to attention on the doorstep. Her face was gleaming, her hair perfectly plaited and the Toilet Tendering Service had done wonders tracking down a new set of Tryton Mell uniform in her size. She looked nothing like Alice Dent.

'You're for it now, Maggott! You wait till Miss Grammaticus hears you're back. Ooooh, I can't wait to tell her; I wouldn't like to be you.'

Alice looked around as Mrs Peasley pulled her inside. Nothing seemed to have changed. It was mid-morning and the hall was quiet – everyone was in lessons. *I'm glad to be back,* Alice thought, and even though she knew she was in trouble, she gulped back a little giggle of happiness.

Then Mrs Peasley cured Alice's giggles immediately.

'Miss Grammaticus is busy right now, but while you wait I've got the perfect place to keep you out of trouble . . .' Mrs Peasley smiled nastily. 'I'm putting you in The Cage.'

The Cage! Alice's heart gave an extra-loud thump. How could she find out the Best Minister's plans if she was locked inside there?

The human-sized cage outside Miss Grammaticus's office was empty. Alice stepped miserably into the thick black bars, her heart sinking into her boots.

'Excellent,' said Mrs Peasley, smirking as she turned an enormous cat-sized metal key. Alice slumped to the floor in despair. *I've failed already,* she thought. *I can't do anything locked in here.*

WHOOSH!

'ARRRGH!' Mrs Peasley shrieked as a cascade of icy water poured over her head, drenching her completely. Startled, Alice leapt to her feet and peered upwards. Oscar and Henry were leaning over the balcony above, sniggering.

'YOU NOXIOUS NASTIES!' screeched Mrs Peasley, running off towards them, dripping water everywhere.

Alice was left alone.

She tried rattling the bars of The Cage, but they wouldn't move. The only way out was by unlocking the door. Alice paused. She didn't think that Mrs Peasley had rushed off with that enormous key.

Hardly daring to hope, Alice slid her hand through the bars towards the lock. And for once her luck was in; the key was still there. Frantically, Alice twisted it until the lock scraped.

She was free!

There was still no one around. Heart thudding, Alice slid out and crept over to Miss Grammaticus's study door. Perhaps there was a clue to the Best Minister's plans inside. Alice reached out to the keypad, her hand trembling.

'"Vile!"' she remembered, and tried tapping it in, but the lock didn't click.

'"Vermin" ... "Vomit" ...' No luck.

Alice couldn't think of any more 'V' words, perhaps Miss Grammaticus had also run out and moved on to 'W'.

'"Worm" . . . "Waste" . . .' Still the lock refused to budge.

'"Wart" . . .'

And amazingly, 'Wart' made the lock click. Giggling a little at this, Alice cautiously turned the door handle and peered in.

Nothing had changed since she was last there, but the room wasn't empty. Alice nearly fainted as a huge black shape leapt up and licked her face.

'Precious! Get down!' she gasped. 'You scared me!'

And now Alice was stuck. In books it always seemed so obvious where to hunt for clues, but this was real life and Alice wasn't sure she'd recognize a clue even if it hit her in the face. She stifled an urge to giggle; this really wasn't the time.

'Where would you look, Precious?'

As if he understood, Precious ignored the clock-lined shelves and padded towards the desk. Alice nodded – yes, that seemed like the best place to start.

But before she reached it there was a deafening click.

Alice's heart nearly stopped. Hurriedly, she dived behind the white sofa nearby, Precious cowering down beside her.

Alice peered out.

All the shelves of clocks were rotating!

Alice jumped. She must be seeing things, or dreaming. Then she realized what was going on – whole sections of the wall were moving.

As she stared, black-uniformed figures poured into the study from tunnels behind the walls and lined up in orderly rows facing the desk. They stood in silence, waiting. Alice thought there must be over a hundred people altogether; it was a good thing the headmistress's study was so big.

Then the door behind the desk opened. Miss Grammaticus walked in, accompanied by a tall man also dressed entirely in black.

Alice's insides turned to ice.

The man's pale face was horrifyingly familiar.

The Best Minister!

Trembling violently, Alice risked lifting her head for a better look – and almost screamed. The Best Minister had raised his head too and she was gazing directly at his deep, dark holes of eyes. They transfixed her. She couldn't move. *Could he see her?*

His eyes dominated his face in the way his height towered over everyone else in the room. Everything about him was black or white; black hair, black eyes, black clothes starkly shocking against his white skin. The only colours were the medals pinned to his chest.

When he finally turned his head, Alice fell limply back against Precious. Relief washed over her. She hadn't been spotted – not yet.

'Are all my troops here?' asked the Best Minister in a cold, sinister voice. Miss Grammaticus nodded.

'Good – I have excellent news for you all; I'm almost ready to seize control of the country. Now listen carefully. At exactly five o'clock this afternoon, you will leave this office to put my great plan into action. You'll start with the children. Tonight, you must take command of the police and get them to grab the dirty little super-spreaders out of their flea-ridden beds. Every single child in the country must be dealt with before tomorrow. Turkey, as my Chief Planner, tell us what's been planned.'

Turkey began to list the plans eagerly.

'Take all children away from their mums and dads immediately!'

'It's the best way to stop parents passing on their disgusting habits to the next generation,' interrupted the Best Minister as the soldiers murmured in surprise. 'Now silence! Carry on, Turkey.'

Turkey continued chanting his plans with relish. 'Lock them up in Ministry-approved schools and don't let them see their families ever again! Make them do lessons every single day from dawn to dusk – everyone not top of their class will get punished! Ban sweets, chocolate, cakes and biscuits – we don't want any more black rotten teeth. We're still working on the plan to pull out all the teeth of children with more than two fillings; there aren't enough dentists.'

'Well, use vets then, they pull out horses' teeth all the time, it can't be much different,' said the Best Minister, looking impatient. 'Carry on, Turkey.'

'No TV or anything with screens ever again – we need the little blighters to concentrate! Daily cold baths – we're not wasting hot water on the little squirts! Cancel Christmas!'

'Yes, I don't get any presents, I don't see why anyone else should,' Miss Grammaticus murmured.

By now Alice was boiling with rage. How *dare* the Best Minister do this? Alice imagined all the little kids being snatched from their beds and having their teeth pulled out. She had to stop him, but how could she? *There's no time – they're doing this tonight!* she thought in panic.

'And when the little horrors aren't doing lessons they'll be litter picking and scrubbing everything clean by torchlight. We've bought lots of tooth-brushes for them to scour pavements with.' Turkey finished with a flourish.

'Excellent!' said the Best Minister. 'That will keep the country nice and clean and make me popular with the public. There's only one flaw. Did you deal with the Dent child?'

Alice jumped, shrinking smaller behind the sofa.

'Errr ... well ... err ... We nearly had her but then she disappeared again.' Turkey's voice trembled. 'And ... err ... err ... she's got the antidote.'

The room was deathly silent.

'Turkey, you have failed me in this, the most important task of all,' the Best Minister's voice was quiet, menacing. 'It's bad enough that the Dent girl escaped me once already without having you fail me too. I have no room for failures. Take him away.'

Turkey shrank against the wall, moaning. Two men stepped forward, picked Turkey up and carried him behind one of the rotating walls. It swung shut behind them.

'Such a shame, but I'm sure the next person I pick to find that wretched girl will succeed,' said the

Best Minister softly. The other grown-ups avoided his eyes, hoping not to be noticed. 'She'll wreck everything if she's not caught.'

'Your excellent plans are both fool-proof and Pirus-proof,' Miss Grammaticus declared. But even she shrivelled under the Best Minister's withering stare.

'Don't be foolish, sister,' he said, 'No plan is Pirus-proof.'

Alice started. Had the Best Minister just called Miss Grammaticus *sister*?

No way! she thought. *There's just no way . . .* but then dawning horror turned her insides to ice.

That photo on Miss Grammaticus's desk!

Alice remembered it clearly, the photograph that Kevin had accidently knocked over – its sinister family in black and white, the dark-haired boy and girl . . . brother and sister . . .

It's true! she thought, suddenly feeling sick. *The Best Minister is Miss Grammaticus's brother!*

Alice pulled herself together. The Best Minister was still talking and she needed to listen.

'Let me explain to you simpletons. This Pirus makes you happy. Once people get it we can't control them because happy people aren't afraid to do what they want. The ones that hate their jobs quit work. The cowardly ones stop being scared of me so don't follow my orders. My plans to take over the world will be wrecked!' As he spoke, his voice started to crack.

'Everyone will stop doing lots of shopping because they won't need expensive things to make themselves happy – that means I won't be mega rich from taxes and can't afford lots of ultimate weapons. But worst of all . . .' The Best Minister stopped, choking with anger, '. . . worst of all, parents will be happiest spending more time with their children, passing on disgusting habits and spoiling the brats for ever. And don't get me started on the damage when children catch the Pirus; the after-effects are so unpredictable that any of them could end up a terrible threat. I can't risk that. When I find the Dent child I will exterminate her – and everyone she's been in contact with!'

Alice had heard enough. The Best Minister's plans chilled her to the bone. She had to stop him. Creeping along behind the sofa, she heard the next person presenting.

'I've got some brilliant slogans to convince parents,' the man said eagerly – and to Alice's relief he darkened the room for his presentation. 'How about "Good Manners and No Play Makes for a Great Day", or "Only a Fool Hates Perfect Pupil School", or "Muddy Boys Get No Toys" and "Grimy Girls are Full of Smells"?'

Despite being desperately worried about the Best Minister's plans, the slogans nearly finished Alice off – they were dreadful! She had to get out before anyone heard her laughing.

Biting her lips to stop giggles escaping, Alice crawled cautiously into the black shadows at the side of the room. Everyone was too busy looking at the screen to notice her and soon she was sliding out of the door.

Safe in the corridor outside, Alice laughed until she couldn't breathe, imagining what Kevin would say when he heard the slogans. But in the end she forced herself to stop. She had work to do.

The corridors were deserted. Alice crept towards Mrs Peasley's office, hoping it would be empty of grown-ups.

It was.

Unfortunately it was also empty of pupils. There was no sign of the others. Alice stood in the middle of the room, puzzled. Mrs Peasley had said they were in her office, but where?

'Oi, up 'ere!'

Alice jumped, her head snapping upwards.

She had found them. Jago, Kevin and Chloe were dangling from the ceiling like model aeroplanes.

'What are you doing up there?'

'Isn't it obvious?' asked Chloe bitterly. 'We've been suspended.'

CHAPTER SEVENTEEN
Stoves Have Ears

Ten minutes later they were all safely in the Dusty Side library.

'Are you OK? What happened?' asked Alice, alarmed, as the others lay groaning on the sofas.

'The police caught us in Saltley Rockpool,' explained Jago. 'Mrs Peasley reported us missing so they knew who we were. Kevin lied about you – he told them Portland Maggott had gone straight home and we didn't know who Alice Dent was.'

'Yeah, then they brought us back so Mrs Peasley could demonstrate what happens to ungrateful children who run away,' added Chloe bitterly.

'Never mind that, did yer get the antidote?' interrupted Kevin.

'Yes, but now we've got an even bigger problem...' Alice told them everything that had happened and what she'd overheard in Miss Grammaticus's study. She left out the part about Principal Swift telling her to destroy the antidote. She still needed to think about that.

By the time she'd finished talking, the others were sitting on the edge of their seats, mouths open.

Chloe spoke first.

'The Best Minister and Miss Grammaticus are really brother and sister?' she said, aghast.

'Frazzling fruitcakes! How are we supposed to fight them both?' complained Kevin.

'Just what I was thinking,' said Jago grimly. 'Two problems, firstly we're not adults and secondly there's no time left to plan anything much.'

'Principal Swift said eleven was old enough!' Alice knew that whatever the other three said, she would have to try stopping the Best Minister. 'If you three won't help me I'll do it on my own!'

'Of course we're gonna help yer!'

'I'm with you too, even if it's hopeless!'

'I didn't say I wasn't going to help!' Jago sounded hurt. 'I was just pointing out how difficult it'll be. And we can't do it alone, we'll need the others and that means taking big risks. You understand this could go horribly wrong and then—'

Kevin interrupted before Alice could. 'Jago, mate – SHUT UP!'

'I'm only pointing out that we're likely to die.' Jago sounded even more hurt.

'This is war, mate, someone's always gonna get hurt.'

'We've got to protect Alice whatever happens,' said Jago. 'She's the best weapon against the Best Minister we've got.'

'And she's our friend!' Chloe added.

Alice fingered the vial in her pocket guiltily. *I'll destroy the antidote when the time's right and tell them then,* she promised herself.

It was Chloe's idea to use their Solutions lesson to make battle plans.

'We need to tell the others anyway, we can't do this on our own,' she said. So, when Mr Pye left the classroom, Jago bent down to Alice, who was hiding inside one of the kitchen cupboards.

'You speak to them.'

'I can't!'

'You'll have to,' Jago was firm. 'And tell them who you really are, so that they listen to you.'

Nervously, Alice climbed out and up on to the hob.

'Portland! Great – now tell us why you were silly enough to come back!' Oscar shouted, grinning. 'I couldn't believe it when I saw you in The Cage.'

'Yeah, that was stupid! The others were dragged back, but you came back yourself – you must be cracked!' Henry added in disgust.

Everyone clustered around Alice, talking excitedly and asking questions about what she'd been doing.

'I'll tell you what happened later, but first I've got to tell you something.' Alice crossed her fingers. She hoped desperately that she was doing the right thing. 'My name's not really Portland Maggott. It's Alice Dent.'

The other pupils gasped.

'You mean . . . that girl on them posters Mrs Peasley put up?' asked Oscar, shocked. 'But you look nothing like her!'

Alice nodded, blushing as everyone immediately stared hard at her.

'The Best Minister's after her because she's got this infectious thingy called a Pirus,' Chloe told them. 'It makes animals really love her. Alice, show them what's in your pocket.'

'The Pirus makes me happy as well,' Alice added as she lifted Nibbles out, but everyone was too busy cooing over the preening mouse to listen. Instead they all wanted to know how they could catch the Pirus too.

'That's enough!' ordered Jago at last. 'Right now, we've got a really big problem. Tell them, Alice.'

'The Best Minister's planning to grab all the children in the country and do horrible things to them and he's doing it tonight,' Alice said, slipping a protesting Nibbles back into her pocket.

Quickly she told them all about the Best Minister's plans. When she had finished, everyone was boiling with rage.

'No one's pulling all my teeth out – no way!'

'I'm not having cold baths – not ever!'

'We've got to stop them!'

'Let's fight them!'

'Yeah, fight!'

'Fight!'

'Shhh! The staff will hear!' Chloe ran to the door and checked outside. Alice held up her hand.

'We can't fight them. They're too big and there's too many of them; they'll turn us into mincemeat. They hate children, don't forget. And if they get scared they'll just disappear back into the secret corridors in Miss Grammaticus's study. We need to get them out of the study to stop them. They're here until five o'clock, so we haven't got much time.'

'That's only three hours away. Anyone got a plan?' asked Jago.

There was silence.

'I know where there's a big tub of ball bearings,' said Kevin at last.

'Yeah, so what?' said Henry.

'Have yer ever tried to walk on 'em?' asked Kevin, a big grin spreading over his face.

'What about the Poppets?' asked Oscar. 'They'll try and stop us.'

Everyone stopped talking. They knew Oscar was right.

Then Emerald screamed and leapt into the air. The stove hob she was perched on was moving. They stared in horror as it flipped open.

'I might be able to help,' said Mr Pye, climbing up through the stove. 'I just need six of your best clothes makers, the sewing machines in the dungeons and a false wig and beard.'

'B-b-but . . .' Alice stammered.

Mr Pye smiled. 'You didn't think I was on the Best Minister's side did you? Why do you think I always let you make such a mess?'

He bent closer to Alice. 'Full marks on your spelling test I think, Alice Dent. And I trust Principal Swift solved your little antidote problem?'

Alice felt her mouth fall open. 'The note? That was you? You know who I am?'

Mr Pye chuckled. 'You lot talk far too much in lessons. Haven't you heard the saying that stoves have ears?'

'Walls,' corrected Jago. 'The saying is "walls have ears".'

'I prefer stoves,' said Mr Pye firmly.

The ideas flowed rapidly after that. Within an hour they had a plan.

At four o'clock, there was a knock on the front door.

'Sanitized Physical Education Supplies at your service!' said the smart black-bearded man with thick glasses who stood on the doorstep. Alice thought no one could possibly recognize Mr Pye underneath.

'We make guaranteed germ-free equipment for getting children fit. Demonstration requested by Miss Grammaticus,' Mr Pye added hastily as Mrs Peasley opened her mouth to tell him to go away.

The Averages hung eagerly out of the upstairs windows and watched as rolled-up plastic packages were taken inside to the main hall.

'Miss Grammaticus wanted her best pupils to test the equipment,' said Mr Pye as a giant fuzzy purple wall rose up from a machine behind him. It looked like one side of a bouncy castle. 'I don't need any help – just keep me supplied with strong tea.'

'I'll leave you to get on with it then.' Mrs Peasley strode away, looking totally miffed.

'I've got a Harvester Trugg, Lewis Berry, Courtney Snell and Freddie Darling listed,' Mr Pye read from a notebook in his hand. 'The instructions say . . . test this to destruction and give me your valuable opinions on whether to buy it, my little poppets.'

He looked up. 'These must be very important and clever pupils – where are they?'

The Poppets gloated as they pushed forward.

Alice didn't dare to believe that Mrs Peasley hadn't even questioned it. She could hardly keep still as the Perfect Poppets were helped into brand-new fluffy (and very hastily stitched) yellow overalls and led across the hall towards what looked like a large cannon.

It was over very quickly. Four rapid shots later and the Poppets were spread-eagled high up on the inflatable wall, held fast by the thousands of tiny hooks coating it. They couldn't move.

Everyone fell about with laughter as the Poppets shrieked and struggled helplessly. Unseen, Mr Pye packed up the rest of the equipment and slipped out.

'I'm going to call an urgent staff meeting,' he whispered to Alice as he passed. 'It'll keep the teachers out of the way.'

Alice couldn't believe how well everything had gone so far. Perhaps there was hope now for the rest of their plans.

CHAPTER EIGHTEEN
The Battle of Tryton Mell

Jago made Alice, Kevin and Chloe meet him on the Dusty Side for a final check through.

'It's ten minutes until five o'clock – is everything battle ready?'

They all nodded.

'Are you sure *all* the staff are out of the way, Kevin?'

'Yeah, I told yer, they're at Mr Pye's urgent meeting – and I . . . er . . . locked the staff room door to keep 'em there.' Kevin grinned, waving the key.

Jago nodded approvingly.

'What about Miss Grammaticus and Mrs Peasley?'

'Still in Miss Grammaticus's study with the Best Minister,' Chloe told him.

'Stop fussing, mate!' interrupted Kevin impatiently. 'Yer know it's all sorted.'

'Yes, all the people-traps are set and everyone knows what to do. Everyone's helping, even the Dunces.'

'Not the Poppets, they're still stuck,' objected Jago, who hated inaccuracy.

Chloe glared at him.

'And I've locked all the animals in the hand-washing classroom so they can't get hurt,' Alice added hastily. 'I've messed up my hair too, so the Best Minister's soldiers know I'm Alice Dent.'

'Are *yer* gonna be OK, Alice?' Kevin asked her. 'Yer know yer need to run like the wind in front of them soldiers and tell the others they're coming.'

'Keep moving and you won't be caught,' Jago advised.

Alice nodded. She wished the boys would stop giving her advice; it made her feel a lot worse.

'Time to go,' said Jago, checking his watch.

They climbed down the chimney one by one. Grinning, Kevin hurried off. He had to remove the giant emergency emptying plug from the bath at exactly the right time; Jago had big plans for the bathwater.

'You go too, Chloe,' ordered Jago, and she sped off.

Jago and Alice picked up the other end of the bath's giant hose-like waste pipe and ran in the direction of Miss Grammaticus's study.

'Good thing I pulled this end out of the drain and hid it here earlier; we've only got two minutes and seven seconds to go,' Jago muttered, as he aimed the pipe towards Miss Grammaticus's study door. Alice couldn't help him much; she was trembling with excitement and nerves.

Very soon, the pipe quivered as the pressure from the released bathwater built up . . . and built up . . .

'Five, four, three, two, one—' A column of foaming water burst out of the diverted waste pipe and jetted towards Miss Grammaticus's study door.

'NOW!' yelled Jago, and Alice flung the study door wide open.

'ARRRGH!'

Scores of soldiers shrieked as torrents of water blasted in. They tried to dash towards the door but fell helplessly, knocked over by the blast.

It was just as if Jago was playing skittles.

Alice grinned, but then the jet of water abruptly slackened and fizzled out ...

'GO!' shouted Jago.

Wet soldiers were surfing furiously towards them. All giggles gone now, Alice stepped forward.

'You want me – come and get me!' she screamed, before turning and sprinting down the main corridor. The soldiers hurtled after her.

It was time to activate the traps.

'They're coming!' she shouted, leaping past the first ambush. As soon as she had passed, the youngest Dunces flung handfuls of ball bearings across the shiny floor.

'ARRRGH!'

'OUCH!'

The Best Minister's troops screamed as they slipped and tripped and crashed to the floor. The Dunces grinned as they tied up the fallen soldiers.

Alice giggled, but didn't dally. She knew that once the ball bearings had rolled away, there was nothing to stop the next wave of soldiers ...

'They're coming!' she screamed at Oscar.

He'd prepared a large lake of golden syrup mixed

with treacle and other things that made it as slippery as ice (it was amazing what they had learnt in Solutions). It was unfortunate for the soldiers that the trap was directly under a large wasps' nest that Alice had cautiously borrowed from the Pest Control classroom. Thanks to the Pirus, the wasps hadn't minded at all when she moved them into the best stinging position, but they were very unhappy about having to share their syrup lake . . .

'Now!' Alice shrieked up to the girls waiting at the top of the secret stairs. They had made battering rams out of giant gym balls filled with water. These shot down the stairs like cannon balls, knocking over anyone in their path.

Some of the troops were stupid enough to try and climb the stairs between the twin slides. A pupil on each chute, a rope between them as they slid down, and the soldiers tumbled to the bottom.

Alice ran on. She was having fun now.

'Get ready, Emerald!'

Emerald had coated the floor with a layer of quick setting jelly. This made the invaders skid and crash together, just like cars on ice.

'They're coming, Henry!'

Henry waved at her.

'I'll get the best score, you wait and see!'

He was right. His rat trap was the best weapon of the battle. It doused passing soldiers in sugar solution and porridge oats then caught them with a tripwire. They fell screaming into the rat pen and disappeared under an onslaught of rats, eager to eat the sweet flakes (rats can never resist oats, no matter who they are attached to).

Giggling, Alice stopped to watch.

'Get lost, Alice!' Henry shouted. 'You're distracting my rats!'

Chloe was waiting in the entrance hall, holding a tin of enormous black spiders and a catapult. Getting the spiders had been easy; Alice had put her hand into a tangle of cobwebs and let the spiders run up her arm. It still made her shudder to think about it.

'Ready?' Alice asked, still fizzing with excitement.

Chloe shook her head. 'I'm really s-scared.' She shook so much that her teeth chattered. 'And my nose keeps running!' She sneezed loudly.

This startled the two Pest Control class rats who were snuffling around Alice's feet. They had slipped over to Alice at the rat trap, clinging to her so firmly that in the end she'd taken them.

'I'm not sure I can do this,' Chloe said.

'You'll be fine,' Alice told her. 'Now give me the spiders!'

'Spiders won't stop the Best Minister's men!' Chloe protested. She had said things like this a lot while Kevin was giving her a crash course in how to fling stones from his home-made catapult.

'Trust me, they will,' Alice retorted, taking the tin. 'Most grown-ups hate spiders.'

'No sign of Jago.' Chloe changed the subject firmly.

Alice had been trying not to think about where Jago had got to. They had agreed that he would look for the Best Minister and come and tell Alice when he was captured. It wasn't good news that he hadn't arrived.

'Shhh! Someone's coming!'

Alice heard it too, the quick footsteps of a lone person hurrying.

'Jago!' she said, relieved, stepping out.

'No, don't—' Chloe tried to stop her.

Too late.

It wasn't Jago.

It was a tall man, dressed in black and frighteningly familiar. For several seconds they both froze, staring at each other, then Alice reeled back in horror as the man's black holes of eyes widened in recognition.

It was the Best Minister!

'Ah – so I've found you at last, Alice Dent,' he said with satisfaction, his terrible voice sending shivers down Alice's spine. 'You've caused me a lot of trouble, child, but that ends right now.'

Alice couldn't reply; her mouth was parched with fear.

'So this is where you've been hiding?'

Alice trembled – the Best Minister's mask-like face was terrifying close-up.

'Trust my idiot of a sister not to recognize you; I'll deal with her later. But first I'll deal with you.'

He casually flicked his gloved hand. To Alice's absolute horror, a long metal pole snaked out of his sleeve and a vicious hook on the end snagged her tunic.

She screamed.

Chloe screamed too.

Alice couldn't move; the metal pole had her in an iron grip and was raising her up off the floor. The Best Minister began to pull her towards him, his dark eyes spearing hers.

'The catapult!' yelled Alice, but incredibly Chloe dashed forward and kicked the Best Minister's shin instead, dropping the tin of spiders on the floor.

'LET HER GO!' shrieked Chloe.

Struggling uselessly, Alice saw that the lid had popped off the spider tin and a few brave spiders were creeping out. She hastily averted her eyes so the Best Minister didn't spot them, but he was too busy terrorizing Chloe to notice.

'You're in *serious* trouble now, girl,' he told her viciously.

Chloe froze, turning deathly white. But her kick had set the rats off. They darted forward, nipping and biting at the Best Minister's ankles. For just a second he looked down, the hook wavering . . . and noticed the spiders swarming up his legs.

'ARRRGH!' he screamed, letting go of Alice and swatting wildly at his trousers. Alice fell painfully to the floor.

'RUN!' screeched Chloe, backing away from the Best Minister, who was now stamping on the spiders.

But by the time Alice had untangled herself, the Best Minister had recovered. He snatched up his hook and reached for her again . . .

'YOU CRUEL MEANIE – they were *harmless*!' Alice shouted as she fled, twisting through corridors at top speed, terror making her faster than a rocket. The Best Minister ran after her, she could hear his harsh breathing coming closer and closer...

Panicking, Alice led him through the battle traps, but he avoided everything. By the time he had ducked under the wasps' nest, Alice was desperate. The other pupils shrank back as she passed, unable to help. No matter how she tried to shake the Best Minister off, he easily kept up with her.

Alice's lungs were bursting; she had to slow down. The gap between them narrowed. He was going to catch her with that hook. It was getting closer... and closer...

'No!' she screamed, as it missed her by a flea's breadth.

Then, a brilliant idea struck her.

'Can't catch me, Beastly Minister!' she shrieked, tugging open the door of the hand-washing classroom. As she had hoped, the Best Minister tore in after her.

'Come and get me then,' said Alice, turning to face him with a big grin.

The Best Minister skidded to a halt.

'You little . . !' he cursed furiously, his black eyes flaming.

All the animals that Alice had locked up in the classroom flung themselves at her in delight. Cuddles, Precious, badgers, hedgehogs, squirrels and a multitude of rodents all pushed against her.

Alice sniffed happily. The smell was disgusting. Even better, she could see steaming piles of droppings everywhere.

The Best Minister choked. Quickly he took out a perfectly folded handkerchief and held it across his face. Alice giggled. She guessed he wouldn't risk getting too close now. He was way too frightened of catching nasty germs.

But even from across the room, he was still terrifying.

'You can't escape me, you horrid little child. I *will* hunt you down in the end – so I'll give you one last chance now. Give me the antidote!'

Alice jumped, abruptly swallowing her giggles. She fingered the vial in her pocket.

'Why do you want to get rid of the Pirus?' she asked, needing time to think. 'What's wrong with everyone being happy?'

The Best Minister's eyes glittered. 'Happy people are dangerous, they just do what they like. I can't *control* happy people.'

'That's horrible!'

'Horrible? *Horrible?* You don't know what you're talking about, you idiot girl! My family lost everything in the last Pirus outbreak. My Great Grandfather caught it and gave away everything: our fortune, our country estate and our family title, just because he was so *happy*.' He made happy sound like a terrible disease.

'Now I've finally got everything back, been made an important Best Minister and was just about to grab even more power, when you show up with your poxy Pirus and wreck everything!'

The Best Minister stopped, his voice cracking. Alice wondered fearfully if he was mad, but when he spoke again, he was calm.

'You can't stop my fantastic rise to power with a few childish traps, Alice Dent. You'll never escape me now, I'm far too important. I know where you are. You can't run from me.'

His eyes bored into her. Alice shuddered.

'I'll squash you like a fly, make no mistake about that. I won't let any spoilt little nuisance live who defies me. Unless . . . unless you hand over the antidote.'

Alice clutched the tiny bottle in her pocket.

'Give it to me, and instead of eliminating you, I'll cure you – I'll waste the first drops of antidote on saving your wretched little life. Don't you want to live, child?'

He held out his gloved hand.

'Give me the antidote!'

Alice couldn't breathe. Nibbles quivered in her pocket, and she could see Precious circling the Best Minister, hackles raised.

Slowly, reluctantly, she took the vial out of her pocket.

'Yes, that's it. Give it to me . . .'

Alice gulped, looked directly into the Best Minister's terrifying eyes and deliberately threw the vial on to the hard floor.

It smashed into smithereens.

The Best Minister's face blanched even whiter. For a moment Alice thought that he might faint. Then he flung out his hook, his mask-like face cracking into rage.

'I'm going to make you *very* sorry you did that, you foolish child.'

As Alice hurriedly backed away, the animals surged forward in a tight pack. The Best Minister tried to fend off them off, but they dodged around his hook and lunged straight at him, jaws snapping. Furniture and sinks smashed as he fought – until in the end, shrieking with fury and disappointment, he leapt backwards and disappeared out of the door.

Alice sat down abruptly in the middle of the hand-washing room as her legs gave way.

I've wrecked the Best Minister's plans! she thought, putting an arm around Precious. She couldn't stop smiling, even though she knew the Best Minister could come back for her at any time.

'Well, look on the bright side, I don't think we'll have to sing the hand-washing song this week,' said Oscar cheerfully, popping his head round the class-room door and surveying the dung covered carnage inside.

The police arrived soon afterwards – Chloe had made the most impressive phone call ever. She told them that Tryton Mell had been attacked and asked the police to hurry please as the pupils had caught the criminals ready for arresting.

The main hall resembled the aftermath of a great

battle. Dozens of prisoners were tied up, all groaning or unconscious. High above them the Poppets were still stuck to the purple wall, goggling at the scene below.

The policeman in charge took one look and got busy on his radio.

'This is the worst thing I've seen! We need back up! Send ambulances! Send fire engines! Send the navy! Send everyone!' And within minutes, ambulances, fire engines, social workers and more police arrived.

'Right, now tell me what's been going on here!' demanded the chief policeman, looking puzzled.

They all tried to tell him the truth at once, explaining about the Best Minister's evil plans and how they had foiled them. But even before they finished, it was obvious that the authorities had already interpreted what had happened to their own satisfaction.

'Sounds like these burglars broke in and threatened the poor children. The little dears did a good job of defending themselves, mind.'

'Over-active imaginations, but that's to be expected at their age.'

Alice nearly burst with rage at this, but Kevin

just shrugged his shoulders.

'Don't yer fret, them grown-ups were never gonna listen to the truth about the Best Minister's plans or believe that a bunch of kids could beat him.'

Jago nodded in agreement with Kevin.

'Strange thing though,' one of the police mused. 'The suspects refuse to say a word and none of them are carrying any identification. That's a criminal charge and a prison spell straight away under the Best Minister's new rules.'

This cheered Alice up a lot. She felt a familiar feeling in her chest.

'I'm going to giggle!' she warned the others. In answer Jago and Chloe sneezed in unison. Alice whipped round and inspected them. They both looked like they had nasty colds.

'I think you're getting my Pirus,' she said, and started laughing as they stared at her in shock.

Everyone lined the corridors and cheered as the prisoners were marched off, handcuffed in pairs. Jago insisted on shaking the spare hand of each prisoner. The police obviously thought he was mad, but Alice knew he was determined to make sure that all the Best Minister's soldiers got the Pirus.

'They won't be able to hurt us then, because they'll be too busy being happy,' he explained.

Alice searched every face, but the Best Minister wasn't there. She wasn't surprised. He wasn't the kind of man to get caught.

There were no teachers either; Alice guessed that they must still be locked in the staff room. But that didn't explain where Miss Grammaticus or Mrs Peasley had gone.

Then, as the police were checking the register, Miss Grammaticus sailed in through the front door, immaculately dressed in coat and gloves.

Alice and Chloe goggled at her. Alice couldn't believe she could just stroll in like that as though nothing had happened.

'How did she escape?' she asked Chloe indignantly.

'No idea, she was in her study with the others. Maybe she got out through one of the secret doorways.'

Miss Grammaticus took one look at the scene and gasped.

'Oh my goodness! What on earth is going on? Can't I leave you alone for one evening without there being trouble?'

'Don't believe her! She's part of all this! Can't

you see she's lying?' Alice shouted, furious that Miss Grammaticus wasn't going to be arrested. Kevin grabbed her, hastily covering her mouth.

'Shut up Alice!' he hissed. 'Yer don't wanna get noticed!'

'Oh, my poor little children!' Miss Grammaticus cried, ice glinting in her eye, as the chief policemen explained what had happened. 'Never mind, I'm here now, and here's Mrs Peasley coming too, so you can go. We'll make sure everything's all right.'

Alice nearly exploded at this, but luckily the chief policeman wouldn't leave until Miss Grammaticus had sent the children to bed.

'Just in case there's any more trouble,' he said, watching the firemen, who were up ladders cutting the weeping Poppets down. 'It's all been very strange, and I don't think we want the children upset by anything else.'

Miss Grammaticus looked very put out, but there was nothing she could do.

'Bed, children!' she called, choking over having to be nice. 'You can skip bath for once, it's so late.'

'Good job, since there's no water left,' said Kevin.

CHAPTER NINETEEN
What Happened Next

As soon as they reached their dormitory, Chloe and Alice scrambled into their pyjamas at top speed.

'Better do what we're told – Miss Grammaticus is *furious*!' said Alice.

'What do you think she'll do to us?' Chloe asked, her voice shaky.

'Probably—' Alice stopped, turning.

The door handle was rattling.

'Oh pants!' gasped Chloe, diving under her covers as Mrs Peasley burst in.

'You're all to go back to the school hall this minute! Them's her orders!'

'What, in pyjamas?' Emerald sounded scandalized, but Alice didn't mind at all. She was very fond of her pyjamas now; they had been through a lot together.

And when they got to the hall, it didn't matter at all because everyone else was wearing nightclothes too.

'Maybe Miss Grammaticus is giving us one of them pyjama parties,' Kevin grinned as he and the other boys slipped over to stand in line behind them.

Chloe glared at him.

'Miss Grammaticus is so mad we'll be lucky if we're still alive by tomorrow,' she said gloomily.

'Yes, but we did get most of the Best Minister's army arrested,' Alice said, trying to cheer her up.

'And hear that screaming? Mrs Peasley's just gone completely nuts – she's found out someone's vandalized her handwashing classroom. She's in there sobbing,' said Oscar cheerfully, winking at Alice, who couldn't help giggling at this.

'But the Best Minister escaped and he knows exactly where to find Alice,' Jago pointed out, which made Alice stop giggling at once.

'Yer worry too much – it'll be fine,' said Kevin as Miss Grammaticus strode angrily to the front of the hall, Precious by her side.

'The police have only just left. They told me that you were attacked tonight. I know better. I know that you nasty snivelling little rabbit droppings attacked those poor innocent people. I want to know who organized it. They are nasty little snoops and must be punished!' Miss Grammaticus's voice rose to a scream. Alice thought she saw steam coming out of her ears.

No one spoke.

'If you don't tell me who led this I'll punish all of you. I'll lock you in the dungeons for ever!'

Alice took a deep breath. There was no way she was letting everyone else be punished for what had happened. This was between her and Miss Grammaticus now. She stepped forward.

'I don't think you should do that,' she said loudly. 'That would be cruel and nasty.'

Miss Grammaticus's eyes bulged. 'Portland Maggott! So it was you! I always knew you were a nasty little worm.'

'And us!'

Alice looked around. Jago, Chloe, Kevin, Oscar and Emerald had stepped forward too. She was very touched, but carried on talking.

'You see, I was in your study earlier, Miss Grammaticus, and I heard you and your brother planning some really nasty things.'

Miss Grammaticus turned puce. 'I'm going to destroy you, you horrid little Maggott!' she shouted, launching herself forward. Precious rose to his feet, growling.

'Oh, didn't I say that Precious was there too? Come here, Precious.' Precious leapt off the stage and stood by Alice, snarling.

'Trugg, get her!' screamed Miss Grammaticus.

'Yeah, Trugg, come and get me!' said Alice, grinning, but Trugg hung back, well out of reach of Precious.

'Do you know who I really am, Miss Grammaticus?'

'A revolting little worm?' The headmistress snarled, glaring at her.

'No, I'm Alice Dent.'

'No . . . NO!' Miss Grammaticus staggered

backwards in terror.

'She's gone red!' shouted Oscar.

'She's gone white now!' screamed another boy.

'And blue!' Henry added gleefully.

Miss Grammaticus slumped to the floor. The Poppets stood back uncertainly, but Alice stepped forward guiltily to check the headmistress was all right.

'NO!' Miss Grammaticus screamed at her. 'Keep away from me, you Pirus-infested menace!'

'Oh I will, don't worry,' said Alice. 'But I think you've already been infected. If not, my friends have just got their Pirus colds. They're very generous, and you know children are super-spreaders, so they're going to share their germs with you. Jago's already shared his with all your friends. They're brewing nasty little colds, and they'll be so much happier soon. I expect they'll share the Pirus with their friends too.'

Alice paused to see what effect her words were having. Miss Grammaticus was curled into a little heap on the floor, moaning loudly. Alice decided to carry on.

'And one more thing, Miss Grammaticus – the last vial of antidote is gone. I smashed it in front of your brother,' Alice told her, grinning. 'So I think you're definitely going to get my Pirus.'

This was the last straw for the headmistress. As she gave a terrible moan and fainted, Alice turned to face the school.

'I think everything's going to be all right now,' she said, beaming.

'Three cheers for Alice Dent!' screamed Oscar.

'Alice! Alice! Alice!' shouted the others.

Alice was carried through the corridors by a crowd of cheering pupils.

'You were amazing,' said Emerald, her eyes shining. 'Just amazing.'

In the entrance hall, everyone threw themselves on the plastic sheeting that covered everything.

'Tear it down!' urged Oscar, demonstrating. Shortly afterwards, Kevin found the keys to the padlocked swings, which made everyone very happy.

'Let's tear down everything!' yelled Henry, rushing off to attack the boarded-up side passages. But before anyone could follow him, the telephone in the red phone box rang loudly.

Everyone fell silent.

'What the . . .' Kevin muttered, diving in to answer it.

Alice held her breath, but Kevin soon shot out again, the biggest smile ever on his face.

'Mum's going to be all right!' he screamed. 'She's going to be in hospital for ages, but they're going to make her better!'

'Of course they are!' said Mr Pye briskly, striding towards Alice as everyone cheered. He shook her hand.

'Well done Alice! I'm proud of you,' he said quietly, and this made Alice glow inside.

'Let's have a midnight feast!' Oscar shouted, grinning.

That feast was the best meal of their lives. Mr Pye, Emerald and Kevin produced mounds of pancakes, sausages, beans, eggs and buttered toast – all perfectly hot and steaming. The happiest bit for Alice though was when the door opened and Principal Swift rushed in, followed (to Alice's great surprise) by the Dr Goodish-Leeches.

Principal Swift smiled at her. 'Alice, you've done brilliantly! See, I told you eleven was plenty old enough to save the world. Thank goodness you're OK!' she said, holding out her arms.

'It's great to see you too!' Alice replied, beaming as the Principal hugged her just like a proud mother would.

'Is the antidote completely destroyed?'

'Completely,' Alice reassured her, grinning.

'Hello Alice,' said the Dr Goodish-Leeches cheerfully.

'What are you two doing here?' Alice didn't mean it to sound quite so rude, but the doctors didn't seem offended.

Dr Diana Goodish-Leech smiled. 'When you visited, we thought the whole thing was very odd, so we went searching for answers. My husband's an expert in communicable diseases and I'm an epidemiologist, so we can make up our own minds about the risks from your Pirus spreading.'

'You're a *what*?' Jago didn't like words he'd never heard of before.

'An eppy … deem … eee … olo … jist,' explained Dr Diana. 'I find the truth about illnesses in facts and figures. It seems that your Pirus has a ninety per cent chance of saving the world if it spreads – given how people behave when they're happy and the Best Minister's plans against children.'

'Wow!' Alice pulled Nibbles out of her pocket

and put him on the table next to the rat twins, who were gazing adoringly up at her.

'How cool is that, Nibbles? It's only breakfast time and I've already saved the world.'

Precious gave a jealous bark. Cuddles broke off from terrorizing the little Dunces to nudge Alice's feet. 'Will everyone attract animals, then?'

'No – not everyone,' Dr Diana replied. 'Last time the Pirus had different effects on different children. We have no idea what will happen this time.'

'Wow! Hope I get to fly!' exclaimed Kevin.

'Don't be stupid!' Jago told him cuttingly. 'Any after-effects will be something physically possible, flying's impossible.'

'You might not get any, if you're totally happy normally then the Pirus only gives you a cold with no after effects,' warned Dr Diana Goodish-Leech.

'That'll be a swizz!' Kevin looked disappointed.

'By the way, Alice,' said Dr Digby Goodish-Leech. 'Your parents were right after all, weren't they? This germ is extremely dangerous. It almost got you killed.'

'I never thought of that,' said Alice, taken aback. 'I really hope they're OK, but I wonder if they'll ever forgive me for getting it?

'I think you'll be surprised – this came to your house for you.' Dr Digby handed her a postcard plastered with exotic stamps.

Alice read the message on the back with increasing astonishment.

Dear Alice,

Hope your Pirus isn't causing you too much bother and those in charge are looking after you. Your mum fancied a trip somewhere hot to shake off these horrible colds we've just had, so we've paddled to Africa in a kayak to build mudbaths for hippopotamuses.

We're so happy here with all the animals – they love having their daily bubble washes and scrub-downs, especially the lions. Your mum's even been keeping those dusting skills in tip-top shape by dusting giraffes. We're not coming back for a while, so do whatever you want.

Dad

'I think we can assume that they've been well and truly infected,' said Dr Digby Goodish-Leech dryly.

Principal Swift smiled.

'Do you mind staying here Alice? It'll be easier for me to keep an eye on you – I'd like to do that.'

Alice beamed at her, but she still had questions. 'What about Miss Grammaticus?'

'Don't worry about Gertriss Grammaticus for a bit, she's petrified with Pirus fright,' the Principal said reassuringly.

'So Mrs Peasley's headmistress now? She hates me even more!'

'No,' another voice chipped in. 'I'll be taking over as temporary headmaster. I put in first dibs in the staff meeting.'

Everyone turned to stare.

'Mr Pye!' A great big grin spread over Kevin's face. 'That's brilliant, sir!'

'A perfect choice,' agreed Jago, nodding with approval.

Alice was delighted too, but she had other worries that needed sorting.

'What about the Best Minister?'

'The Best Minister's men are all in jail. He got caught out by his own laws there. He can't carry out his plans – he won't risk getting his soldiers released if they've been infected by you lot. And he won't dare to come for you himself without the antidote, so for the time being, he's not a problem.'

Kevin grinned. 'That's great! So we can take Alice to the beach now and build sandcastles together – we promised her.'

Alice beamed at him.

'What a lovely idea!' said Principal Swift. 'May I come too? I'll get my bucket and spade.'

'But what about Professor Tryton?' asked Chloe. 'Is he OK?'

'No one knows where he is,' Principal Swift told her. 'But don't fret, the Professor can look after himself; I'm sure he's safe. He's tough and very resourceful – he'll only be found when he wants to be.'

'And we've still got Mrs Peasley to deal with!' Chloe was working down her own list of concerns. 'She'll be even worse now she's been passed over for headmistress!'

'Oh, don't worry about her,' said Alice, stroking Cuddles. 'I'll only let her have Cuddles back if she's nice to everyone.'

As everyone laughed, Principal Swift held Alice's gaze.

'So you'll stay?'

Alice turned to look at Jago, Chloe and Kevin, who were coughing, sneezing and smiling all at the same time. They were her friends now, she couldn't imagine not being with them.

'I'd love to stay,' she said and then added, giggling, 'I want to be here when Miss Grammaticus gets the Pirus!'

ACKNOWLEDGEMENTS

Creating a book is like setting off on a big adventure. And like many good adventures, this one started with a mysterious phone call late one chilly January evening. It was Barry Cunningham, who told me that the wonderful reader Laura Myers had picked out the first draft of this story from all the entries in the *Times*/Chicken House competition (thank you Laura!) and I had made the longlist.

I didn't make the shortlist (this was probably a good thing, getting what you want is often very bad for you), but Barry asked me if I'd like to work with Chicken House to refine that first manuscript into *Alice Dent and the Incredible Germs*. A huge thank you, Barry – and of course I said yes!

The middle of any adventure is always the hardest part, and when you're writing a book, you need good editors (these are a little bit like good teachers). The best editors advise you how to polish a story until every page shines. Even more importantly, they do this in such a nice way that you end up liking them a lot. I've had two of the very best editors, Kesia Lupo and Rachel Leyshon, and I want to tell them how fantastic they are.

Then there's Rachel Hickman, who really understood how this book should look on the outside so that everyone would want to read it. A massive thank you goes to her and also to the cover designer Steve Wells and illustrator Sarah Horne, who drew the brilliant picture on the cover.

After a final polishing (thank you Claire McKenna and Victoria Walters!), all books need to reach the people they were written for. So I'd like to thank Jazz Bartlett, Elinor Bagenal, Laura Myers, Esther Waller, Sarah Wilson, and everyone else on the Chicken House team for making sure that, whatever the Best Minister for Everything Nicely Perfect might have wanted, as many people as possible now know about the Pirus.

And finally, I'm really grateful to you for reading this story. This was probably a wise move, because next time you get a terrible cold you now know what might happen, especially if you start giggling helplessly a few days later . . .